DOCTOR WHO

ADVENTURES IN LOCKDOWN

BBC

DOCTOR WHO

ADVENTURES IN LOCKDOWN

Edited by Steve Cole

BOOKS

BBC Books, an imprint of Ebury Publishing
20 Vauxhall Bridge Road,
London SW1V 2SA

BBC Books is part of the Penguin Random House group of companies
whose addresses can be found at global.penguinrandomhouse.com

Contents

Publisher's note

Stories 1–4, 8 and 10–11 were first published on the official *Doctor Who* website as part of a lockdown initiative led by Chris Chibnall.

Stories 5–6, 12–13 and 15–16 first appeared online as part of the *Doctor Who*: Lockdown! series of watch-alongs organised and produced by Emily Cook

Stories 7, 9 and 14 were written especially for this collection.

The publishers would like to thank Chris Chibnall, Russell T Davies, Steven Moffat, Emily Cook, the *Doctor Who* brand team, the Children in Need team, and each of the authors and illustrators for their contributions to this book.

1

A Message from the Doctor

Oh, hi!

This is an emergency transmission. If you're reading this, the TARDIS must have detected an upsurge in psychological signals from somewhere in space and time – basically, I think somebody somewhere might be a little bit worried.

I'm actually just self-isolating – or, as I like to call it, *hiding* – from an army of Sontarans. But keep that to yourself. Now. Here's what I do in any worrying situation:

1. Remember, you will get through this. And things will be all right. Even if they look uncertain. Even if you're worried. Darkness never prevails.

2. Tell jokes. Even bad ones – especially bad ones. I am brilliant at bad ones.

3. Be kind. Even kinder than you were yesterday. And I know you were super kind yesterday! Look out for each other. You won't be the only one worried. Talking will help. Sharing will help. Look out for your friends, your neighbours, people you hardly know, and family. Because in the end, we're all family.

4. Listen to science. And listen to doctors, right? They've got your back.

5. Stay strong, stay positive.

You've got this. And I will see you very soon.

The Doctor

2

Things She Thought While Falling

by Chris Chibnall

She was cold.

The Doctor was cold.

The ragged clothes weren't helping. She was cold, and in someone else's ragged clothes.

She felt a little peeved that the ragged clothes did not include a built-in parachute. That felt like an error.

Wait, she thought. *Why would I want a parachute? Oh yes, that's right.* She remembered.

She was falling.

Air was rushing past her. Or, more accurately, she was rushing past air. Tumbling through the cold night sky.

Also, she was fizzing.

Remnants of regeneration particles were still skittering off her. The process was still… in process. Her newness still in train.

The Doctor looked up, mid-plummet. *Oh dear,* she thought.

Far above her, the TARDIS was exploding.

That is very unhelpful, she thought.

No, wait, not just exploding. Now the TARDIS was dematerialising – while it exploded. *Dematerialexploding,* thought the Doctor. *That's not a word,* chided the Doctor. *All right,* replied the Doctor, *I'm only a few minutes in here – you're lucky I've got any words at all. Will you two stop arguing,* chimed in the Doctor. *Only if you stop subdividing us,* replied the Doctor. *This is all the same brain. Don't confuse matters.*

As the blue box vanished, leaving the Doctor looking up at a starry black sky, the Doctor wondered if she'd ever see her TARDIS again. *No time to feel sorry for yourself,* she told herself. *Too much going on!*

Yes, she thought. *There is a lot going on.* A large dark painful ground mass was rapidly approaching, and inside the Doctor's body her cells continued to burn and reshape and reform.

Well, thought the Doctor. All of her. *This is a conundrum.*

Her newly minted mind had already had three thousand and seven thoughts over the course of three seconds. She knew because she had counted, and she only realised she'd counted once she'd finished counting, and then she wondered whether the counting made three thousand and eight thoughts and then she realised that the ground was another second closer, and a plan would probably be in order.

She saw the ground and calculated her own velocity. *Ooh, this is going to hurt,* she thought. *Even with a soft landing. And it probably won't be a soft landing.* She crossed her fingers and hoped she was heading for an open-air trampoline factory.

Like that planet, what was it called, Fintleborxtug! Fun fact about Fintleborxtug, she told herself, *the creature that named it did so when it was hiccupping and just before it was sick. Nobody knows if it was really the name or just the sound it made.*

You don't have to tell me that, thought the Doctor tetchily to herself. *I know! I know the planetary surface of Fintleborxtug is as soft and bouncy as a trampoline, because I went for a long bounce there once, among the mountains and the purple sky. I'd just had ice cream sundaes. That was a mistake.*

Can you please concentrate, the Doctor thought to herself again.

She concentrated. She confirmed she was still falling. Disappointing, but not that much of a surprise given her circumstances hadn't changed in the second since she last checked.

She wondered where exactly she was. Which sky she was falling through. Which ground she was heading for. She stuck her tongue out. It was buffeted by the air. Tickled. Ah. That tasted like Earth. Northern Europe.

Britain. Wood smoke, diesel, grass, fast-approaching concrete, lot of moisture and attitude in the air. Yorkshire. Possibly South Yorkshire.

She snuck another look down. A train track. A stationary train. She tried to recognise the livery on the outside of the train so she could absolutely nail precisely where she was, but it was distant and dark and regeneration had once again failed to deliver the super-powered, see-in-the-dark, X-ray vision she had always craved. *Ah well*, she thought, *maybe next time.*

Now the train below was insisting on getting even closer. The train or the tracks were where she was going to land. She pondered her limited choices – tracks would hurt. Mouth full of gravel and two big metal lines all the way down her new body. Ouch. Train might be better – the roof, if she could crash through it, would soften her landing a bit (though smashing through was most likely going to hurt a lot).

With a bit of luck, any injuries would be taken care of by the still-fizzing regeneration process. Like those injuries the Doctor had got after he'd crashed through the roof at Naismith Manor. Or the hand he'd managed to grow back after the Sycorax had lopped one off. *Watch out, Doctor*, she thought. *Your personal pronouns are drifting.*

That roof was super close now. She flapped her arms a bit to make sure her trajectory was bang on. As she did so, she saw that the train lights were out. She saw sparks of a light flashing in one carriage towards the back of the train. Something was wrong. And if something was wrong, she was the man to sort it out.

You're assuming you're going to make it through this fall alive, she reminded herself. *Now, don't be gloomy,* she chided back. *Things will be all right. Right now, they're not ideal. But I can muddle through. Probably.*

That's interesting, she thought. *I seem to be an optimist. With a hint of enthusiasm. And what's that warm feeling in my stomach? Ah, I'm kind! Brilliant.*

This is going to be fun, thought the Doctor, as she crashed through the roof of a train, on the outskirts of Sheffield, not far from Grindleford.

Then, having hit the floor of the train, and felt extra little regenerative energy particles heal where things had scratched and broken and hurt – newness, in train, on a train – she thought to herself: *This is going to be a very interesting night!*

The Doctor jumped up, zapped a creature she couldn't quite understand and immediately made new friends.

3

The Terror of the Umpty Ums

by Steven Moffat

The reeking flesh mass was silent for a moment before twisting and stretching its upper, frontal skin lumps into a new configuration. Karpagnon's visual circuits processed and pattern-matched the configuration within two nanoseconds: apparently the human was smiling. Karpagnon considered for a moment and elected not to retaliate.

'Did you hear me?' emitted the Human from its flapped aperture. 'Did you understand? Do you understand what I'm saying?' The encoded sound stream was accompanied by a fresh flow of smells also emanating from the aperture. Karpagnon's sensory filter began processing the new odours, while his tactical monitor noted that they were unlikely to be directly significant to the Human's communication. The light spray of moisture was similarly dismissed. 'I'll be back tomorrow morning. Dr Johnson and Dr Ahmed will be here too. Do you remember them?'

No explicit threat detected, noted the Tactical Monitor, while the Strategic Oversight Junction added that an implied, non-explicit threat was still possible – but then the Strategic Oversight Junction was like that. *Beef and onions*, advised the Sensory Filter.

Karpagnon scanned the habitation box again, but there was no new information of tactical value. There was the little bed (which he had to pretend to sleep in) the window (which was barred) and the door (which was open at the moment). His scan ended on the Human (*Dr Petrie*, proffered a Context Activated memory bubble), who was sitting on the chair by the bed and clearly expecting a reply. Karpagnon sifted among the options presented by his various Diplomatic Interface Modules and selected appropriately. 'Yes,' he said, 'I received and understood your communication and I remember Dr Johnson and Dr Ahmed. I shall destroy your world and all who breed here in fire and anguish. I hope you enjoyed your beef and onions.'

'I'll be seeing you, then,' said Dr Petrie, and rose to go.

'I shall eviscerate you at the first opportunity,' replied Karpagnon. 'Good night.'

As Dr Petrie moved to the door, the Tactical Monitor advised: *Escape must be initiated in 2.7 hours in full darkness.*

The Strategic Oversight Junction further advised: *All humans in the installation should be destroyed before departure. The human designated as Dr Petrie is the priority target.*

The Sensory Filter noted: *The sweat gland emissions from the human designated as Dr Petrie reveal significant adrenal content. This indicates Dr Petrie has a fear reaction in the upper quartile.*

'And a big bottom,' added another voice.

If Karpagnon could have frowned, he would have. Where did that come from? He did a quick internal scan but couldn't source the unexpected data stream.

'I mean you wouldn't expect it from the front, but then he turns round and boom!'

'Identify untagged data stream!' demanded Karpagnon.

'I mean, size of that thing! Could take your eye out.'

'Identify untagged data stream!' repeated Karpagnon.

No untagged data stream detected, replied the Internal Data Relay Monitor.

Karpagnon considered for a moment. The additional stress of maintaining his holographic shell (currently projecting an image of a 12-year-old boy called David) could conceivably be causing glitches in the logic junctions. Perhaps it was no more than that. A temporary shutdown would fix the problem, and in any event it would be wise to refresh his systems before the escape.

For appearances' sake, Karpagnon swung his legs round so that he could lie down on the bed and switched his hologram eyes to the closed position. As he lay there, he listened to his internal relays shutting down one by one.

Tactical Monitor going offline.

Strategic Oversight Junction going offline.

Sensory Filter entering sleep mode.

Internal delay on alert mode only.

For a moment there was only the ticking darkness.

'N'night, fam!'

The Karpagnon awoke. According to his chrono-register, 2.7 hours had passed. He swivelled his head to look at the window and confirmed that darkness had fallen, then got up from the bed and checked his hologram status in the mirror. The shell was holding. He waited a moment, allowing his systems to come on line. As usual the Tactical Monitor was first.

Recommendation. Human casualties to be avoided during escape.

Karpagnon noticed his hologram shell was frowning in the mirror, which was odd because he didn't know it could do that. 'Sorry, could you repeat your last recommendation?'

Human casualties to be avoided during escape, repeated the Tactical Monitor.

In the mirror the hologram shell was looking positively bewildered, which was definitely a new feature. 'Why?' asked Karpagnon.

New protocol, replied the Tactical Monitor. *Cruelty and cowardice to be avoided. Destruction of humans within this installation now designated as cruel and cowardly.*

'What new protocol?' demanded Karpagnon.

'Oops, sorry that was probably me.'

It was the voice again – the untagged data stream. But where was it coming from?

'I got bored, you see,' the voice continued. 'Thought I'd do a bit of housekeeping, long as I'm here. Love a bit of rewiring, me, and I get bored when I'm asleep. I can't be doing with all that sleeping, there's too many planets. What if you sleep and miss a whole planet. Nightmare, yeah?'

'Who are you?' demanded Karpagnon.

'Just a friend, who wants to help. We're doing an escape, right? I'm *top* at escaping.'

'I require no assistance,' said Karpagnon. 'Strategic Oversight Junction, please run a diagnostic on the Tactical Monitor. There seems to be some kind of interference.'

Karpagnon waited but there was no response. 'Strategic Oversight Junction, please run a diagnostic on the Tactical—'

Can't we at least discuss this? asked the Strategic Oversight Junction, with a new tone in the digital overlay that could only be described as cross. *I mean, why has it always got to be what you say? What if anyone else has an opinion? Did you ever think about that?*

'Oh dear,' said the voice. 'My influence, I'm afraid. You see, I do like a flat management structure. Always run one myself – from top to bottom. Obviously I have to be top. No offence to anyone else, it's just a thing.'

'You are interfering with my systems??'

'Tell you what, I'll just switch them off, shall I? Then we can get on with escaping.'

There was a soft clicking as Karpagnon's internal systems started shutting down.

'Who are you??' Karpagnon demanded.

'Shouldn't we be getting on with it, the escaping? Time to start sneaking downstairs, I think.'

'Who are you and what are you doing in my head?'

'Well who are *you* and what are you doing in this place?'

Karpagnon was about to refuse to answer the question, when, to his surprise, he found himself answering the question. 'I am Karpagnon. A DeathBorg 400, warrior class. I was forged in the weapon groves of Villengard, and I am on a surveillance mission on twenty-first-century Earth.'

'In a children's home?'

'The details of my assignment are forbidden knowledge.'

'Well I better not ask you about it in case you start telling me everything for no particular reason.'

'I am not so compliant,' snarled Karpagnon. But he couldn't help noticing he had left the room and was now sneaking down the stairs – just as the voice had wanted him to.

'DeathBorg 400,' she was saying. 'Did they have 399 before you that didn't work out? It's not a reassuring number, is it?'

'Who are you?' he asked.

'Oh, Karpagnon, you know who I am. You've known all along.'

'Tell me!'

'I'm the Doctor.'

Karpagnon came to a halt four steps from the foot of the stairs. Had he been programmed for any kind of shock, he would have been experiencing it now. *The Doctor!*

'Ooh, look at your memory banks lighting up! Heard of me, then?'

Heard of her? 'The Ka Faraq Gatri,' replied Karpagnon. 'The Oncoming Storm, the Bringer of Darkness, the Imp of the Pandorica! The final victor of the Time War.'

'A few of my hits. I'm glad you've been paying attention.'

'You are known to many as the greatest warrior in the universe.'

'I'm not a warrior, but have it your way.'

'How can you be in my mind?'

'What if I were to tell you, I'm talking to you through an earpiece?'

Karpagnon rapidly processed this intelligence. 'How could my defences be breached and an earpiece applied?'

'Wrong question.'

'How could an earpiece rewire my internal logic relays?'

'Still the wrong question.'

Karpagnon reached up to locate the earpiece, but –

'*Don't touch it,*' snapped the Doctor. 'Touch the earpiece, and this is over. I will not help you.'

'I do not take orders!' thundered Karpagnon – though he couldn't help noticing he'd lowered his hand. 'Why would a DeathBorg 400 need your help?' he protested, in a slightly higher register than he really intended.

'Because you want to get out of here,' replied the Doctor. 'Which is fine by me, because I don't want a DeathBorg 400 wandering around a children's home. The front door is 20 feet in front of you, shall we get going?'

'First I must destroy this installation, and all humans within it.'

'It's not an installation, it's a children's home.'

'First I must destroy this children's home and all the humans within it.'

'Well that seems a bit mean to me, but OK. Better go to the kitchen, yeah?'

'Why the kitchen?'

'It's where they keep all the burny stuff. You know where the kitchen is, don't you, Karpagnon?'

'Of course!' Karpagnon descended the rest of the stairs and headed through the shadowed, silent corridors to the kitchen.

'Why are you so afraid of humans?' asked the Doctor.

'I do not fear humans. I despise them.'

'Oh, come on, I'm sitting in your ear, I can see your whole brain. Of course you fear them.'

'I hate all humanity.'

'Yeah, but that's the point, isn't it? You hate them. Hate is just fear out loud.'

'I know nothing of fear,' said Karpagnon, as he entered the deserted kitchen.

'Well I know everything. I'd have to, me. What with the Daleks, and the Cybermen, and the Weeping Angels.'

'These creatures are known to me.'

'Of course they are, everyone's scared of them. And the Sontarans and the Slitheen. And of course, the Umpty Ums.'

Karpagnon scanned his databanks twice. 'The… Umpty Ums?'

'Oh, they're the worst. Nothing scares me like the Umpty Ums.'

'They are unknown to me!'

'Oh, if you know about me, you know about the Umpty Ums. But never mind that now. We're in the kitchen! What are we actually going to do?'

Karpagnon stood in the middle of the large, dark kitchen and found himself reluctant to do anything at all. Finally he said, 'This house must burn.'

'Oh, do you think so? Isn't that a bit much?'

'This house must burn,' he insisted, louder this time.

'All the people will burn too. That's a bit unfair. There's a lot of kids here, you know.'

'I care nothing for humanity. *This house will burn.*'

'But the thing is… you don't really want to do that – do you, Karpagnon?'

Karpagnon scanned his Function Drives. It was true, he was detecting… what was that? Reluctance? Had this strange, prattling woman, who was also the most dangerous warrior in the universe, interfered with his base programming?

'Do you want to know *why* you're reluctant, Karpagon?'

'I am not reluctant,' he lied.

'Strategy! That's all. Proper military strategy. I mean, you're a DeathBorg 400 on an undercover mission on planet Earth – burning this house down will only draw attention to you.'

Karpagnon considered. 'Correct!' he declared.

'So. Here's a compromise. Instead of burning the house down, why don't we… *turn the heating up really high!*'

'The heating?'

'Yeah. That'll show 'em! They'll be sweating all night, the human fools! Oh, those sheets will be dripping.'

'But I require vengeance,' protested Karpagnon. 'Vengeance isn't turning the heating up.' But he couldn't help noticing he'd already twisted the heating control dial right up to maximum.

'Well done, Karpagnon! They'll know better than to mess with you in future. Now let's get out of here and leave these puny humans to get uncomfortably hot!'

'No!' said Karpagnon.

'Oh, come on! This escape is taking forever. I mean, I like to draw them out a bit, but this is ridiculous.'

'First I must destroy the human known as Dr Petrie.'

'Oh, OK. If we must, we must. Let's pop along and destroy Dr Petrie, then. Where would we find him this time of night?'

As usual, Dr Petrie had been working late in his office. When Karpagnon slipped silently through the door (maximum stealth mode), he saw Petrie sprawled in his chair, with his head hanging over the back. He was snoring so heavily it almost seemed to rattle the teacup on his desk. Under the teacup Karpagnon noticed a scatter of papers, mostly with photographs pinned to them. The photographs were all of David – Karpagnon's hologram disguise.

'Well then, what shall we do with him?' asked the Doctor. 'Melt him? Miniaturise him? Random phase his atomic structure? I don't really know how to do that last one, but it sounds cool.'

Again, Karpagnon found himself reluctant to act. What was wrong with him? He hated Dr Petrie more than any other living thing – and he hated quite a lot of living things.

'Why do you hate him, Karpagnon?'

Karpagnon hesitated. 'He… humiliated me.'

'Oh, I don't think he meant to. He was trying to help. Remember, he thinks you're a little boy called David with a dissociative personality disorder. Not a DeathBorg 400 from the weapon groves of Villengard.'

'David is a fiction.'

'Oh, yeah, course he is. I know that. But you see, you put so much detail into the disguise. Abandoned by his parents, all those people being so cruel to him… I don't think Dr Petrie was humiliating you, I think he was trying to help. He just didn't know you were a DeathBorg – you must get that a lot.'

'No matter. I will not be pitied, I will have my vengeance. He will be destroyed.'

'Fair enough. Your call. On you go, then – melt away.'

But once again Karpagnon found himself strangely reluctant to act. And Dr Petrie just kept on snoring, louder and louder.

'You know what the problem is,' said the Doctor at last. 'It's strategy again. If you destroy Dr Petrie, it will draw attention to you. You can't blow your cover like that. So what we need is another clever compromise.'

'What do you suggest?'

'Well. Instead of boring old destroying him, why don't we do the one thing human beings really can't stand? Why don't you… go with me on this… *draw a moustache on him!*'

'Drawing a moustache is not proper vengeance,' said the DeathBorg 400 as it reached for a marker pen.

At last the front door stood in front him – unguarded, noted Karpagnon, with grim satisfaction. Freedom was now only inches away.

'What are you waiting for?' said the Doctor in his ear.

Karpagnon reached for the door handle. Hesitated.

'Don't worry, it's quiet out there,' said the Doctor. 'No Cybermen or Daleks. Not even a trace of an Umpty Um.'

Karpagnon steeled himself and opened the door. The cold air filled his lungs. The wind rushed in the trees, and distantly there was the sound of traffic. The sky was packed with clouds but the moon peeked through.

'Lungs?' said the Doctor. 'What do you mean lungs?'

Karpagnon took another breath. So cold. He found himself shivering.

'How can you have lungs if you're a DeathBorg 400? DeathBorgs don't have lungs.'

A cat was slinking along a wall. It glanced at Karpagnon and flicked out of sight. The traffic sighed, and a train rattled, and the wind stirred in his hair.

The Doctor's voice was gentler now. 'Close the door, David. You'll catch your death.'

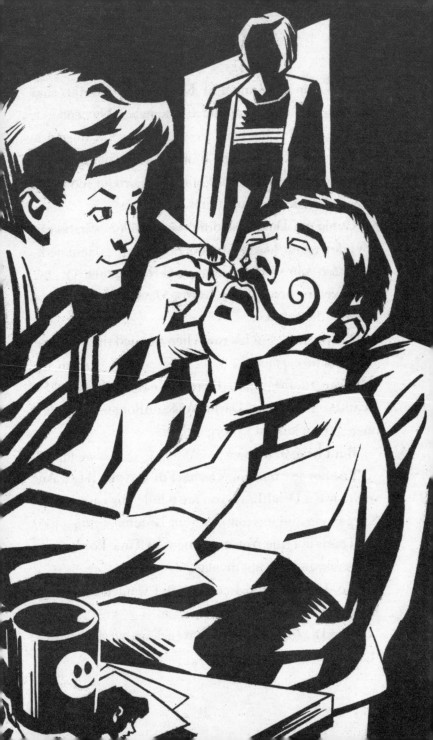

'No!' roared the mind of Karpagnon. 'No, this shall not be!' He strode out into the night. The concrete was freezing on his bare feet and the wind tugged at his pyjamas. He stumbled to a halt, and found himself rooted to the spot. He wasn't programmed for terror, but somehow he was feeling it now.

'Come on, David,' said the Doctor. 'You understand now, don't you? I know you do!'

'Cease your words of lies!' cried Karpagnon.

'If you're tired of my words, David, why don't you take out the earpiece.'

David reached to his ear. Then he tried the other ear. 'There is no earpiece.'

'More to the point, there *are* ears. Why would a DeathBorg have ears, David? A DeathBorg with ears and lungs? What kind of cyborg is that?'

'But I hear your voice.'

'I'm not in your ear, David. I'm in your head. And you're not a DeathBorg, you are a little boy called David Karpagnon and it is *way* past your bedtime.'

'This is not true. You are using your Time Lord powers to disable and corrupt my data systems.'

'No, I'm not. And I couldn't if I wanted to. Do you know *why* I couldn't, David?'

'The Doctor is known to have telepathic skills beyond those of ordinary mortals.'

'Who told you that? How do you know so much about me? Where did you learn it all from?'

'I…'

Karpagnon broke off, as a terrible truth unfolded in his mind.

'I…'

It couldn't be true. It simply couldn't. And yet, as he stood there in the cold and the dark, he saw that it was as true as anything ever could be. He took another breath of the freezing air and said the words out loud: 'I watched you on television.'

'Yeah. Great show, isn't it?'

'*Doctor Who.*'

'That's the one. That's me. But I'm not allowed to call myself that on screen. I don't know why, it's a *brilliant* name.'

'You're… not real.'

'Well not in the limited sense of real, no. But I kept you straight tonight, didn't I? I'm real enough for that.'

'You're a character… in a TV show.'

'Yes, that's right, I am. But really, I'd like to direct.'

David stood in silence. He barely felt the cold now.

'Do you like the music, by the way? Always scares me. *Umpty-um umpty-um, umpty-um umpty-um.*'

'I don't understand…'

35

'Well it's a scary noise, isn't it? I always get wound up when I know I'm about to hear it. That's why I start shouting towards the end of episodes.'

'But how can you be in my head?'

'I go where there are monsters to fight. We've been fighting monsters tonight, you and me. You see, that's the story of the music, I always think. The *Umpty-Ums*, that's the noise of the monsters. But then it goes *Woo-Hoo*. I think the *Woo-Hoo* is me riding to the rescue.'

'You can't rescue anyone. You're just a story.'

'We're all stories in the end. But do you know what a story is, David? It's an idea. And do you know what an idea is? It's a thought so big and so clever it can outlive you. It can fly out of your head, and into other people's. Like I'm in your head, right now. Keeping you right. Never cruel, never cowardly. Always the Doctor.'

David sighed. He was starting to feel the cold again. He looked back at the house, which suddenly looked so warm.

'It won't be easy,' said the Doctor. 'None of it will be easy, ever. But I'll always be there.'

David walked back into the house, went up the stairs, and got into bed.

A few hours later David woke up and stared at the ceiling for a while, thinking about things.

'I get very scared sometimes,' he said.

'*Woo-hoo,*' said the Doctor.

4

Doctor Who and the Time War

by Russell T Davies

This was never meant to exist.

Way back, maybe early 2013, Tom Spilsbury, the editor of Doctor Who Magazine, *asked me if I wanted to contribute to* DWM*'s great 50th special. Maybe addressing that huge gap in* Doctor Who *lore, how did the Eighth Doctor regenerate into the Ninth?*

I said well, yeah, no, but, isn't that best left to the imagination? If I write a script, it would be too real, too fixed, too canonical. But Tom's never one to give up. He said okay, what if you wrote, say, the final pages of a Target novel? About the last days of the Time War. The Doctor's final moments. And we could present it like a surviving fragment of the Novel That Never Was, so it exists in that half-real space of the spin-offs, possible but not factual, just slightly canon, if you so choose.

Okay, Tom. You temptress. I'm in.

41

So I wrote this. It even starts mid-sentence, as if you've just turned to the last pages. Lee Binding created a beautiful cover. We were excited! And then Tom said, I'd better run this past Steven Moffat, just in case...

Oh, said Steven. Oh.

How could we have known? That The Day of the Doctor *would have an extra Doctor, a War Doctor? And Steven didn't even tell us about* Night of the Doctor, *he kept that regeneration a complete surprise! He just said, sorry, can you lay off that whole area? I agreed, harrumphed, went to bed and told him he was sleeping on the settee that night.*

So the idea was snuffed aborning.

Until 2020. When a science fiction-shaped virus came along to change our lives (honestly, I've written the end of the world 100 times, but I never imagined everyone just sitting at home). Emily Cook of DWM *created the livestream of* The Day of the Doctor, *then turned to* Rose, *and asked me if I had anything to offer...? At exactly the same time, Chris Chibnall emailed me, saying we need the Doctor more than ever these days, and could I think of any material?*

By some miracle this file still existed. And then, like a story within a story, I discovered that this chapter was nothing to do with Tom and DWM *after all! My memory had become a blurry spinning vortex. Truth is, it was actually written for BBC Books and was going to be part of their 50th Anniversary book,* The Doctor: His Lives and Times. *Lee still had his illustration (naturally, because he was under a Binding contract, oh I'm so funny). And strangely, looking back, it's funny how things fit; the Moment is described here as oak and brass, which isn't far from the final idea (I don't mean Billie). I wonder; I suspect, without realising, if Steven and I were both riffing off Eighth Doctor-style designs, maybe…?*

More importantly, the idea has come of age. This chapter only died because it became, continuity-wise, incorrect. But now, the Thirteenth Doctor has shown us Doctors galore, with infinite possibilities.

All Doctors exist.

All stories are true.

So come with me now, to the distant reefs of a terrible war, as the Doctor takes the Moment and changes both the universe and themselves forever…

but the Daleks and the Time Lords scream in vain, too far away to stop him now. And so the Doctor stands alone.

He looks out from his eyrie, across the wreckage of a thousand worlds. Below him, fragments of the Time War, broken reefs of Gallifrey and Skaro washed up into this backwater, to rot. His creaking wooden platform shivers with ice, a mile high, atop fragments of Morbius's Red Capitol, its vile towers fused into the black, friable spires of Yarvelling's Church. And yet the Doctor can see glimpses of Earth. The planet had been replicated a million times, to become the bullets fired into the Nightmare Child's skull, and now splinters of human society have gouged themselves into the wasteland below – relics of Mumbai, shards of Manhattan, a satire of Old London Town. Remnants of better days.

The Doctor looks down.

Her skeleton lies at his feet. The bones relax into dust, and she is gone.

The Doctor looks up.

In front of him, at the edge of the platform, a brass handle, mounted in a simple oak casement; the only remaining extrusion of the Moment into this world, the rest of its vast bulk hidden, chained to an N-form, churning behind the dimensional wall. Screaming to be used.

He steps forward. He grips the handle. He wonders what his last words should be. He decides that last words are useless. He pulls the handle down, flat.

The Moment happens.

The universe sings.

The war ends.

Surrounded by brightness, the Doctor sees the sky above parting to reveal, just as Bettan and the Deathsmiths of Goth had predicted, the final event. Gallifrey Original convulses and rolls into flame. Its concentric rings of Dalek warships become silhouettes, then ashes, and then –

The Doctor falls. Every atom around him is sucked upwards, towards the fire, but he alone is capable of falling, saved – or damned – by the Moment's shadow. Above him, he feels the Time Lock solidify, sealing off the war from reality, and as his body tumbles out of existence, into plasmaspace, then foulspace, then beyond, the Doctor leans into the fall, head first, arms wide, diving into infinity.

Alone.

Except…

There.

Something else.

Falling.

Spinning…?

A whirl of blue. That faithful blue. Then a rectangle of white, widening, a doorway, coming closer, towards him and, as the grind of ancient engines reaches a crescendo, he thinks: I'm going home.

The Doctor lies on the TARDIS floor. His bones broken from the fall, his hearts hollowed by his loss. Around him, the console room

buckles, warps, shudders, still suffering from the High Council's resurrection of the Master, long ago. It aches for a new shape. 'Me too,' mutters the Doctor with a grim smile, though he knows regeneration is impossible. The Moment has fixed his existence, and this life is his last.

He wonders what age he's finally reached. The Time War used years as ammunition; at the Battle of Rodan's Wedding alone, he'd aged to five million and then regressed to a mewling babe, merely from shrapnel. Now, the ache in his bones feels… one thousand years old? Well. Call it nine hundred. Sounds better.

Darkness swills through his mind and he forces a smile, ready and yet never ready for the end. Still, no final words.

But then…

Can it be…?

He feels it once more.

That old, deep stirring in every bone and muscle and thought. The joy. The terror. The change, the impossible change!

Amazed, he lifts up his hand. Stares, fascinated, as the skin ripples with a curious new gold.

Of course. She tricked him, right at the end. Her final kiss was not a goodbye; she imprinted the Restoration within him. His lifecycle has been reset, the new man lurching outwards to be born. So this is the meaning of her final song: a whole new body to expiate the guilt. He might even pass the Restoration to another, one day.

Suddenly, they come, in a rush, his final words. He says them aloud, but there is no one to hear, allowing them to be imagined and imagined again for ever.

Then his nuclei turn into stars.

Every pore blazes with light. A volcano of thick, viscous energy cannons from his neck, his hands, his feet, his guts, his hearts, his soul —

It stops.

The Doctor sits up. The new Doctor, next Doctor, now Doctor. He lifts up his new fingers to touch his new head. His new chin. His new nose. His new ears. He takes a deep breath into his new, dry, wide lungs. He says his first word.

'Blimey!'

5

Rose: The Sequel

by Russell T Davies

Chapter 21

Revenge of the Nestene

One little bit survived.

A tiny nugget of Nestene Consciousness lived on. It had escaped the Doctor's anti-plastic by hurrying into the substrata and hiding inside the nearest available shape. The body of a clown.

Days before, the Nestene had posted sentries along the Embankment in the form of living statues, those strange humans who decide to earn a living by dressing up as clowns, robots or statues and then standing perfectly still, waiting for people to throw money at them. What an odd, odd species. But now the plastic guards had dissolved, except for one. A white-faced Pierrot. Well, half a face. Half a head, its right half, a crescent of head perched atop a ruffed neck and glittering silver bodysuit, with one eye, bright as insanity, and a bisected leering grin.

The Half-Head Pierrot hauled itself up onto the opposite bank of the river and looked back at the grave of the Consciousness.

The secret underground lair had collapsed, causing the whole of the London Eye to tilt forward and collapse into the Thames. Pods had broken free, bobbing on the surface, little people inside banging on the glass and screaming for help. The Half-Head half-smiled as the pods were caught in the suction as water poured down into the vast underground chasm, a whirlpool swallowing the pods and people and screams, down, down, down, gone.

'Good!' said the Pierrot, or tried to say, but this only resulted in a gout of dirty water jetting out of its open, plastic throat.

It turned around to look at the remnants of London. In every direction, fires burned, and bodies lay in the streets, victims of the glorious invasion. The immediate area remained flooded, overwhelmed by the tsunami resulting from the Eye's collapse. The streets of Westminster had become a stinking swamp.

The clown stood tall upon the rubble. Overlooking floating cars and fallen buses and weeping survivors, as it formulated…

A plan.

It had to survive.

To survive, and conquer this world.

And more than that. To survive and conquer and then destroy the Doctor. Oh, but to defeat a Time Lord would need extra strength and greater cunning. Perhaps, thought the Consciousness, an alliance? A combination of the Doctor's greatest enemies, perhaps even the mighty empires of Daleks and Cybermen combined, to rid the universe of this pestilence.

An excellent plan.

But then – a spasm of pain, stabbing its plastic guts. The Nestene was dying. Its single cell could not sustain for much longer.

But it knew it contained the energy for one last reconfiguration. If it burnt up its clown molecules in a final polystorm, it could plasticise itself into a new, albeit hollow shape. But what?

Ahead, there lay a palace. The ruins of this little country's government, river water still pouring out of its shattered windows. Inside, amongst the nation's crowns and sceptres, the Nestene might find something it could use.

The silver clown lurched to the opposite side of the bridge. A woman looked at its half-head and screamed. The clown pushed her over the balustrade and she fell, with a wail. It staggered on. Its single eye staring, furious, fixed on the clocktower. The palace seemed to be calling to the Nestene, summoning it to the halls of power. Here, the creature would find its own kind, surely.

It clambered over fallen masonry, waded through stinking pools, swatted aside screaming humans, fuelled onwards by memories. Remembering the day Nestenia fell.

Not so long ago, the seventeen planets of the Plastic Conjunction had been at peace. After aeons of war, the Nestene Consciousness had abandoned the old ways, and entered into rapport with the Embodiment of Gris. Joy and harmony prevailed! The food planets churned out ample supplies of smoke and oil; the Crown Consciousness basked in happiness, its ever-changing shape writhing in a pit of plastic gold. The Embodiment showered it with favours. Some said the Nestene had found love at last.

And then the skies opened.

Onto hell.

It was, the legends said afterwards, the edge of a Time War, a battleground beyond comprehension. A tumble of planets fell out of a rip in space, like stray bullets from some epic offstage gunfight. Copies of planets, stolen from different seconds of their existence; a hundred orange worlds, known as Gallifrey, a thousand black cinders once called Skaro, a dozen small blue-and-green planets which the Nestene recognised from an old campaign: Earth. A rolling, tumbling, spinning, bouncing cosmic destruction unfurled, the food planets smashed by many Skaros, the Crownworld pulverised by various Gallifreys, the Maternity Reefs crushed by 57 Earths.

And then, beyond physical destruction, time itself advanced as a weapon. A wave of Early washed over the Consciousness, reducing it to helpless baby tendrils. A cloud of Late reduced the foodstocks to dust. A blizzard of Tick-tock sent the Embodiment insane.

All in one second.

And then it was gone.

The war was sucked back into its breach, beyond the normal universe, leaving only silence. The ruins of Nestenia and its empire lay glinting in the light of a cold and dying sun.

'No more,' thought the staggering Pierrot, as it entered the ruins of the palace. 'No more!' The Nestene had sworn revenge after the

Time War, deliberately targeting this ridiculous Earth. But now to be defeated again, by a Time Lord and human together…! This time, its revenge would be brilliant. And ruthless. And subtler than anyone could guess, even if it took fifteen years or more.

It had reached the interior corridors. A wet green carpet underfoot. The building had been rotting, long before today's disaster, and sections of both roof and floor had now caved in. The Thames mingled with the stink of open sewers. It seemed appropriate, somehow.

But again, that stab of pain. The cell of Consciousness dying. Time was running out, as the clown shambled onwards, and then…

A body. On the floor. Crushed by a concrete beam.

And yet, the clown felt something in the substrata. A scent, a shiver, a lingering promise from the human's form. Reeking of things which the Nestene recognised. Ambition. Lust. Greed. Joy. Power.

The clown grinned. A grin so wide, its half-mouth split apart and the top of its head fell off. But the now-eyeless quarter-headed Pierrot was unstoppable. Giggling from its throat-tube as it crouched down. It held the hand of the body and began the final process,

Transformation!

The clown began to glow, its atoms becoming furnaces. And the human glowed, its cells separating to feed the ferocious polystorm.

In a swirl of bright particles, the Pierrot ceased to be, and the human scattered away into nothingness.

And something new took shape.

It stood proud. Alone, in a dark, wet, wrecked corridor. A new, true Auton, cradling the last of the Nestene Consciousness within.

A perfect, plastic copy of the human male.

It turned to consider its reflection in the broken glass of an interior door, its substrata probing the remains of the mammal's memory. He had power, this man. He had authority. He had the potential to go so much further.

The Auton smiled at himself. Loving this new self. The suit. The body. The face.

The blond hair.

Oh, this was going to be fun!

6

Rory's Story

by Neil Gaiman

SCRIPT TITLE

Written by
Name of First Writer

Based on,
If Any

Address
Phone Number

DOCTOR WHO TWITTER INTRODUCTION FOR
THE DOCTOR'S WIFE.

INT. RORY'S HOUSE - DAY. OR NIGHT.

Hello Arthur. So, the idea of this
is it's Rory Williams, eight years
after he was sent back in time to
1938. So it's 1946.

And because you're doing this at
home, wear anything you can that
could conceivably have been worn
in 1946. A white shirt and tie,
or a string vest, or (if you don't
have anything knocking around)
DON'T WORRY.

And shoot it against a blank wall
if you can. The idea is that Rory
is dictating his biography

                    RORY
          So. Hullo baby Anthony. This
          is Rory Williams, dictating my
          book for you. I'm not actually
          known as a writer. My wife,

your new mum, Amelia - Amy - she writes the Melody Malone books. You'll read them when you're older.

RORY (CONT'D)
So. It's 1946. And even knowing how the war was going to turn out, I'm glad it's finally over. And I'm mostly impressed by people. They can get through so much, just by being brave, and optimistic, and resilient. Next week, little Anthony, you'll be coming home, here, to me and your new mum. Which is why I'm recording all this for you, on the only working smartphone in the world.

RORY (CONT'D)
Right. In previous chapters, I've talked about how I met your mum, at school, about 43 years from now. How we got engaged. How I was killed by an old lady alien but

69

it was a dream. Then how I was killed by a Silurian and stopped existing completely. How I was a Plastic Centurion waiting for your mum for about 2,000 years. And then how the universe ended and I died again.

RORY (CONT'D)
Then we got married and then I was shot on a dam, and then I drowned, but I was rescued by a mermaid, and your mum gave me CPR. Which brings me to the chapter that follows. In which your mum had to deal with me getting very old, and angry, and, well, dead. Right.

RORY (CONT'D)
So. This is the next chapter of what happened to me and your mother when we used to hang around with... your future brother-in-law. I call this chapter: 'I'm the Pretty One.'

Amy (off) shouts, via the magic
of technology:

> AMY (O.S.)
>
> Rory! Stop faffing about in
> there and come and help me
> paint the baby's room!

And Rory shuts off the camera...

7

One Virtue, and a Thousand Crimes

by Neil Gaiman

The Corsair ran down the dusty stairs as fast as she possibly could without losing control and tumbling headfirst, followed, in a stately and much more dignified way, by a large, levitating metal-and-leather box, slightly bigger than a coffin.

They were in the City Obsidian, deserted and forbidden these last hundred years or more, in the Imperial Edifice of Infinite Steps. The steps were, in truth, finite, but there were an awful lot of them. It had taken her hour after weary hour to walk up them. Going up them, though, had been easier than running down.

The stairs were of volcanic glass, they went down for a very long way, and nobody, the Corsair reflected, as she went down them in a headlong sort of run, ought ever to go down them at a headlong run.

But there was an army close behind her. Not the kind of army that you'd actually want to have behind you, shouting things like 'We'd follow you into battle or anywhere, Corsair,' or even 'Don't worry! We've got your back!' This was the other kind of army: the kind someone would normally deploy, if that someone was, say, Supreme Leader of several inhabited star systems, against the inhabitants of a very small planet that was really, deeply irritating them, with instructions to the army not to come back until the small planet was an even smaller lump of utterly uninhabitable rock, and with explicit orders to leave no survivors. Only in this case, the army wasn't being deployed against anything as big as a planet, but just against one woman with an impressively plumed hat, running as fast as she could down an almost endless flight of stairs…

'Honestly, I should be flattered,' the Corsair had observed, precisely ten minutes earlier, as the first of the troopships had descended from the stars on a pillar of fire.

She had been in one of the topmost rooms in the tallest tower of the Imperial Edifice when the army landed. She had just attached a small silver box to the wall, trying cosmic cheat code after cosmic cheat code in an attempt to open the door of the final room.

'Flattened, more like,' her parrot had replied gloomily. 'What did you think was going to happen? You set off an alarm in a forbidden city on a planet that's off-limits, and that's local security arriving to drag us outside and make us miserable. Let's get back to the *Esperanza*. Now.'

The parrot was a glorious blue from its hyacinth-blue wings and tail to its dusty deep blue head, with a golden yellow splash around each eye. The Corsair, in contrast, was dark brown of skin and unlikely scarlet of hair. Her coat was viridian green, her clothes of tan leather and dark-cherry-coloured velvet were patched and battered. The plumes in her tricorn hat were hyacinth blue, and had been donated by the parrot following its last moult.

'Nope. Not leaving yet. Job's not finished,' said the Corsair. 'The Hand of Omega isn't going to steal itself.'

'Whatever this Time Lord is paying you,' said the parrot, as it watched the troopships land, 'it honestly isn't enough.'

'This particular Time Lord is going to pay me with the satisfaction,' said the Corsair, with a smile, 'of a job well done.'

The parrot was still trying to come up with a sufficiently unimpressed reply when the silver box blinked and beeped to inform them that a cheat code had worked. Simultaneously the far wall faded from existence, to reveal an unlit room on the other side of it, containing what appeared to be a large leather steamer trunk.

The parrot fluttered off the Corsair's shoulder and landed on the steamer trunk. 'Is this it?' it asked, unimpressed.

'Yup. The Hand of Omega. Very important. Stellar manipulator. You can turn a star inside out with this little rascal.'

Parrots can't sniff, they don't have the nasal equipment for it. Still, the parrot performed a perfect impression of the sniffing noise the Corsair made when she was told something she was not going to allow herself to be impressed by. The Corsair tried her best not to smile, and failed.

'Right,' said the Corsair. 'Back to the *Esperanza*!' She tugged, with all her strength, at one of the steamer trunk's handle-like protuberances. The trunk moved perhaps a couple of millimetres.

'Mm,' said the parrot, unimpressed. 'I'm not sure how we're going to carry that down several miles of stairs. And when I say "we" here, I mean "you", because I won't actually be carrying anything. It's the wings. And the load-bearing capacity.'

There were loud booms from outside: hundreds of transporters, each transporter filled with scores of soldiers, were blasting towards them from the troopships.

'Maybe we should, y'know, leave the box here and just fly for our lives,' said the parrot. 'It's not worth getting dead over.'

'Next time round,' said the Corsair, thoughtfully, 'or perhaps the time after that, I want a body with muscles. Big. Strapping. Made for hauling things. With one of those faces people just trust.'

She made no move to leave, though. She just stood and stared at the heavy box. She kicked it, hard, and hurt her foot through her boot.

'You're not helping,' she said to the box.

'I'm advising you on a sensible course of action,' said the parrot. 'They'll be here in a couple of minutes. Let's run!'

There was a crackling noise and a ghost appeared in the centre of the room, drained of all colour: an elderly male with white hair and a black fur hat. The hat rose to a triangular peak. The figure flickered, looked around the room irritably, and then focused on a corner that didn't actually contain the Corsair.

'Do you, um. Have the, the thing yet?' it asked the empty corner.

'I've got it. I just can't move it. It's heavy,' said the Corsair. 'You didn't mention that it was going to be heavy. I would have brought movers. I'm thinking about just pushing it out of the window.'

'Good gracious me. Don't do that. Whatever are you thinking of? You could destroy the continent! Have you tried talking to it?'

'Talking to it?'

'Yes. It's sentient. More or less. It will certainly appreciate being addressed civilly, young lady. Politeness costs nothing.' He pulled a pocket watch from the pocket of his long, black coat. 'But hurry up. We are running out of time.'

'We're Time Lords,' said the Corsair. 'We have all the time there is.'

'No excuse for wasting it then,' said the elderly gentleman testily. He crackled, momentarily, in black and white, and vanished.

'That's your client?' asked the parrot.

'Yup.'

'Doesn't look the type. Looks much too respectable to be a receiver of stolen goods.'

The Corsair smiled. She had a remarkable smile, when she deployed it, whatever body she wore. 'Looks,' she said, 'can be deceiving. Especially when it comes to our customer. Oh, he's a bad boy, that one. He's about to steal a Type 40 TARDIS. And then you won't be*lieve* the trouble he'll get into.'

The window shattered. Someone was firing at them.

Which reminded her.

'Um. Would you mind very much following me back to my ship?' she asked the leather box.

It continued to lie heavily on the floor.

'Please?' she added, as politely as she could.

Somewhere at the back of her head something that was not her felt like it was, reluctantly, waking up.

The box rose an inch, wobbled, then levitated, steadily, into the air, and remained there, unsupported, four feet above the ground.

'Now what?' asked the parrot, fluttering off the steamer trunk and circling the room.

'Now,' said the Corsair, 'we run!'

She ran. The parrot flew ahead of her. The Corsair looked back, to see the steamer trunk hanging unmoving in the air behind them. '*Oy!*' she shouted.

The trunk swayed in the air, as if trying to make its mind up about something, and then, smoothly, it followed them.

Above them, on the tower roof, the Corsair heard thumps and crashes. The building shook. Troop transporters were landing...

The Corsair ran down the dusty glass stairs as fast as she could, in a sort of controlled plummet. Not, she decided, the wisest way to descend. It was a broken neck waiting to happen, and this would be the worst possible time for a regeneration – not that there ever seemed to be a good time.

At the next landing she stopped for a moment, to catch her breath. The parrot circled above her.

The leather steamer trunk caught up with her and waited obediently beside her.

Below them, a window shattered. She heard shouted orders, the sound of many booted figures running up the stairs towards her.

She looked at the battered outside of the large steamer trunk. Inside it was the long-lost Hand of Omega: the fabled stellar manipulator of the earliest of the great Time Lords, technology that could turn any star into a supernova, that could rearrange the very fabric of the universe itself. She grabbed a handle with one hand, pulled herself up onto the trunk. It bobbed gently in the air, like a rowing boat, as she clambered on it.

'Stop! Drop your weapons,' shouted a voice from above her. 'Or we shoot.' Someone shot at her then, to make sure that she understood.

The Corsair didn't have any weapons to drop, unless you counted the Hand of Omega, which wasn't the kind of weapon they were thinking about.

She remembered where she had left the *Esperanza*, envisioned the little sloop in the under-cellar, tried to remember exactly the paths and staircases she had walked from her ship to where they were in the tower.

The Corsair called to the parrot, 'Get under my coat! Now!' The parrot dropped onto her shoulder, and edged into her coat, its blue and yellow head peering out from her collar.

The most powerful thing in this part of the universe purred impatiently beneath her.

'Right,' she said, drawing a map in her mind for it of the staircases in the Imperial Edifice of Infinite Steps, and the journey down to the sub-cellar in which she had left the *Esperanza*. 'Let's go home.' And then, to be on the safe side, 'Please?'

More shots, from above this time.

The steamer trunk moved cautiously through the air, as if it was getting used to being ridden. Then it picked up speed, sliding through the thin air faster than the Corsair had thought possible. The Corsair could feel both of her hearts pounding in her chest with excitement and delight, and she shouted, 'Wheeeeee!' as they lurched around a corner and slammed down yet another staircase.

'You really aren't getting paid *anything* for this job?' asked the parrot, as the steamer trunk crashed through a squad of armed soldiers, sending them flying back down the steps. By the time the soldiers had picked themselves up, the trunk was a tiny dot far below them.

'Not exactly,' said the Corsair. 'I mean, I've already *been* paid. The Doctor got me out of some rather sticky trouble, and so I promised I'd do a job for her in return.'

'OK… and so we're bringing this thing to her?' asked the parrot.

'Of course not. We're taking it back to the fellow in the Astrakhan you saw projecting his eidolon into the room up there. He knows he needs the Hand of Omega, doesn't quite know the reason, has no earthly idea why he has an overwhelming urge to take the Hand to Earth and hide it there, but he expects he'll figure it out sooner or later.'

'Will he? Figure it out?'

'Yes. Much, much later, though. Then he'll use it to send a star nova and incidentally start a Time War. Not *the* Time War. Just a little one. The little one will get erased by the big one. And then nobody will remember it at all.'

'*You* remember it,' said the parrot. '*You* remember everything.'

'The snake,' said the Corsair, 'swallows its tail. And we all wind up where we began.'

'As you say,' said the parrot. 'But I fail to see what your tattoo has to do with… STOP THIS THING I SAID STOP IT OR WE ARE DOOMED!' For the Hand of Omega was aiming itself for the floor at the bottom of the steps, and it did not appear to be slowing down. The parrot closed its eyes, while the Corsair braced herself for a collision and was surprised when the heavy glass paving stones that made up the floor shimmered and dissolved.

'Hand of Omega,' said the Corsair to the steamer trunk, 'you are full of surprises.'

It did not reply, but, for a moment, the Corsair felt a wave of perfect smugness waft up from the steamer trunk and wash over her. The roof reformed above them.

'How did the Hand of Omega get to the City Obsidian in the first place?' asked the parrot, as they drifted on their steamer trunk through the cellar-darkness. 'It's the last place you'd expect to find a long-lost Time Lord stellar manipulator, isn't it? In a hidden room in an abandoned city.'

'Good point,' said the Corsair. 'Probably I'll need to hide it there a few hundred years ago. We'll need to steal it from Omega and Rassilon and the other bloke first, of course. *That's* going to be interesting. Still, they've never met this body before. Might give me the element of surprise.'

She let go of the handle, slipped off the steamer-trunk onto the cellar-floor, and walked forward in the darkness. The parrot edged carefully out of the coat and back onto the Corsair's shoulder.

They were in a lightless cellar, in the centre of a deserted city – abandoned and forgotten amid a dry and barren desert, but the Corsair smelled saltwater, and heard a sail flap in the breeze, and she knew they were almost home.

'Light, *Esperanza*,' said the Corsair, and the little piratical sloop was illuminated by tiny lights that twinkled and shone and danced across her deck and vanished high into the rigging. Far above them, in the building, something went boom, and something else crashed and reverberated. The Corsair strode up the gangplank.

'Right,' said the Corsair to the steamer trunk, which had followed her onto the deck. 'You settle down by that hatch over there, and we'll be casting off in moments.'

The trunk settled on the deck as if it weighed nothing at all.

'Did you miss me, dear?' asked the Corsair as she took the helm. She gripped the ship's wheel in her hands, felt *Esperanza* growl happily under her touch. The *Esperanza* was a model 60 TARDIS: she was old – the Corsair liked to think of her as *vintage* – and she lacked the refinements of modern vehicles, but she was still the best ship there was. There was a *whumpf* as the winds of space-time filled *Esperanza*'s sails, and billowed them out into the nothing-at-all...

A swarm of lights flickered over Esperanza's deck and mast like demented fireflies. There was a grinding, dematerialising sound, like the sound of a universe in pain, and the TARDIS was gone.

Moments later an army transporter crashed into the cellar, and a number of soldiers looked around in puzzlement, seeing nothing out of the ordinary of any kind, apart from a hyacinth-blue feather. They took the feather back with them to their Supreme Leader, who sent images of it across the star system, along with messages pointing out that a healthy reward would be paid for information leading to the capture of the owner of the feather.

The reward would not be collected for several years, not until a strapping big fellow marched up to the Supreme Leader's throne room, with information he claimed would lead to the capture of both of the owners of the feather – the woman and the bird.

The Supreme Leader, who prided themselves on being an excellent judge of character, trusted the man immediately. He had the kind of face that made you want to trust him, after all. A really honest and good-natured smile.

The Supreme Leader paid the reward in full, and even gave the strapping big fellow the feather – to use, the big fellow explained, to bait the trap. And neither the blue feather, nor the reward, nor the strapping big fellow with the snake-swallowing-its-tail tattoo on the inside of his left wrist, and nor for that matter the contents of the Inner Treasure Vault of the Imperial Treasury have been seen since.

But as the poet Byron wrote, somewhat earlier (according to one way of looking at the universe) or much, much later (if you were inspecting the universe from a different direction):

> *For him they raise not the recording stone —*
> *His death yet dubious, deeds too widely known;*
> *He left a Corsair's name to other times,*
> *Link'd with one virtue, and a thousand crimes.*

Lockdown 2020
Isle of Skye

8

The Simple Things

by Joy Wilkinson

Graham wasn't keen on bucket lists. He didn't want to be ticking things off as if there'd come a point where he'd had his fill, and he knew that, when the darkness loomed, he found as much solace in the small things – watching the garden birds, dusting Grace's frog ornaments, hiding the TV remote from Ryan – as he would in bungee jumping off the mountains of Mars.

But when the Doctor offered him the chance to go wherever and whenever he wanted, he knew exactly what to ask for. A small thing, and yet the biggest – a simple kickabout with the first West Ham team to win the cup.

He'd dreamed about it for years. A quick trip back to the glory days of 1964 to tackle Bobby Moore on the training ground. Graham was fully prepared to fall flat on his face in the mud. It would be an honour and a privilege. But this… this was just bloody typical!

'That TARDIS hates me,' Graham despaired. The TARDIS had turned up in a noisy, filthy factory corner, nowhere near Bobby Moore.

'That's weird,' said the Doctor, checking the sonic.

'No it's not. It's exactly what I'd expect. It's been like that ever since I brought my own cushion along, as if it's a personal criticism. I tried to explain – it's memory foam—'

'No, it's weird because we are in the right place,' she managed to cut in. 'West Ham. Monday 20th April, 1896.'

'Did West Ham even exist in 1896?' Yaz asked, trying to give a stuff about football for Graham's sake.

'The place probably did, but not the football club,' said Ryan, who had tuned out as much of Graham's West Ham trivia as he could, but had unwittingly picked bits up.

'No, hang about…' gasped Graham, his eyes starting to sparkle. 'Listen.'

They tried to, but it wasn't easy to hear anything with the CLANK-CLANK-CLANK of the factory racketing on.

'This is an ironworks – that's what they were called at first – Thames Ironworks FC. That's why they're

called the Hammers.' Graham's heart was CLANKING now.

'Surely it's Hammers because of the Ham?' Yaz said.

Graham shot her a withering look, but was soon sparkling again as he figured it out. 'I never said which cup, did I? So it's brought us to our first ever final against Barking – the Charity Cup. Last rematch after drawing twice. We win the trophy 1-0 in our first ever season – today!'

'Keep it down, Granddad,' warned Ryan. 'If the players are around, you don't want to give the game away. If you jinx it and they lose, you'll change the club's whole history.'

'Did they play here in the Ironworks?' Yaz risked another withering look, but Graham was too enthused to admonish now.

'No, but they worked here, so they must be having a last kickabout before heading to the match. I take it back – I could kiss that TARDIS. I'm going to train with Charlie Dove!'

'Or maybe not.' The Doctor was suddenly grave. 'What does this place make, Graham?'

'Ships, mostly. Thames Ironworks and Shipbuilding Company, if memory serves.'

'Warships?'

'That's right. For the Navy. And some other countries—'

'How about for aliens?'

He stared at her. They all did. She wasn't kidding. They followed the trace the sonic had picked up, through the heat and cacophony of the ironworks to a large door that led into a vast workshop. Or that would have done, if it weren't locked. A group of young men were hanging around outside, clutching a ball. Graham went quiet, like a shy little kid. The Doctor was still troubled – as were the men.

'Have you got us locked out?' said the man with the ball. 'It's the only empty space. We need to get in and practise, but the boss won't let us because of some big customer.'

The whole team glared at them, suspicious of the strangers who seemed to fit the 'big customer' bill.

'Don't worry, I've got a bone to pick with them too. Wait there, won't be a tick.' The Doctor sonicked the lock and slipped inside. Yaz and Ryan followed, with Graham last, eyes riveted on his heroes, still unable to speak for fear he might only be able to squeak.

The gigantic room was indeed completely empty, until the Doctor revealed what was behind the perception filter. A leviathan of a spaceship. Iron-wrought like a First World War dreadnought, but a very different shape, tooled for intergalactic skies not seas. Turrets rose on all sides, ready to be decked with alien armaments. A hundred cannons at least.

'Draconian Galaxy-class battlecruiser,' the Doctor breathed in horror. 'Early model, but I guess it's another seven centuries before they use them to wage war on humans. I didn't know you'd crossed paths yet.'

Before the others could get her to break that into bite-sized chunks, another door opened and a man in a suit entered with a tall reptilian humanoid woman in a green robe. The gang needed no help to figure out that this was the boss with the big customer, who wasn't happy to see them sniffing around her gunship. Before the Draconian could declare war, the Doctor was ready with her gambit, for once not even needing to fib.

'Morning! I'm the Doctor – your fifteenth Emperor made me a noble of Draconia. That's all right, no need to bow, just tell me what on Earth you think you're doing building gunships here on Earth?'

The Draconian frowned, but took her at her word and answered simply, 'Where else should we build it? Our civilisation is too advanced to have our own people do such lowly labour. Our specialists will install the high-tech weaponry and systems, but the basic toil is best left to the basic species. It makes perfect economic sense for us both.'

The boss blushed at being dismissed as primitive and was keen to keep face. 'Why wouldn't she come here? We're the best shipbuilders on the planet, and we're almost bankrupt. I'll take work wherever we can get it rather than see our people starve.'

The gang waited for the Doctor to lay into them both, to tell them the warship would be used against humans one day, and that any warship used against anyone was not good, and that humans weren't expendable and exploitable by any empire that rocked up with a poxy chequebook... but the Doctor could see that the boss cared about his men, and that the Draconian was just a procurement clerk, and that warships would always be built by poorer worlds and used by richer worlds to destroy each other, and all of a sudden this nice day had nosedived and she felt the darkness loom and then she said –

'Brilliant! Makes perfect sense... except that I've brought my mate Graham here to have a kickabout with the guys waiting outside, so would you mind letting them in for fifteen minutes? Go on, you can stay and watch if you pop your perception filters back on.'

Graham never knew if it was the fifteenth Emperor's honour or just the coolly authoritative way she said it that won them over but, before he knew it, the ship had vanished, the Draconian woman turned into another man in a suit, and soon the whistle was blowing and he was playing footie with Charlie Dove, and all the lads, booting the ball around the vast workshop, with

Yaz and Ryan standing strategically to stop it hitting the ship.

The Doctor watched alongside the Draconian, commentating in such a way as to pass on all the fundamentals (including the offside rule) and a whole heap of passion, so that when the time was up, the ground was laid.

'Mind if I have this?' She stopped the ball on a rebound and booted it to the Draconian, who picked it up, curious.

'Such a simple object,' said she – or he, as the big customer guise appeared. 'And yet, it's quite fascinating. May I take this back with me to show the Emperor?'

Charlie Dove was about to protest – as was Graham, who'd hoped for a souvenir – but the Doctor cut in once more. 'Please do. You never know, it might help you beat more people than a warship.'

She grinned. So did Graham, realising what she was up to. He reassured Charlie that the team would be fine without their lucky ball and gave them his West Ham pin instead.

'West Ham FC? That's a good name for a team,' said Charlie. 'Shame it's taken.'

'It's not – yet. I – uh – made it up. You can have it if you want,' Graham stammered, as the prototype

Hammers thanked him and headed off to their match – to win the cup.

'Thank you!' Graham shouted, in the TARDIS, to the TARDIS, and to the Doctor and the universe, and whatever else had conspired to allow him to christen his favourite team. Who needed a bucket list when life could twist and turn and surprise you like this on a Monday morning?

The Doctor smiled. She doubted a quick kickabout could ever lead to saving the Earth, but sometimes the simplest things were the greatest things – like her favourite race, and like those beautiful, perfect spheres, on the pitch and spinning in all the solar systems. And if she'd learned one thing about the future, and the past, and the present, it was that she never really knew what would happen next. Which was why hope would always win.

9

The Tourist

by Vinay Patel

Enthusiastic, self-motivated individual required for exciting franchise opportunity with a well-regarded city-based tour-guide company to urgently fill unexpected vacancy. Must have a love for arcane history and for entertaining domestic and international audiences alike. Access to own printer a bonus. Lanyards provided on request.

The absurdity of applying for a job as a tour guide in a place you've never visited, let alone lived in, *had* occurred to George. Who was he to venture out into the big city and immediately slap his authorial stamp on it? OK, so Gloucester wasn't exactly the *big* city, but it was a big *enough* city for George, thanks very much. Sixty-seven years he'd had in this life. Sixty-seven years spent living in the middle of nowhere with his mum, which, to him,

GLOUCESTER

Scale of ¼ Mile

Scale of Metres

0   100   200   300

was sixty-seven years well spent. He didn't want to be here at all.

But it was all different now. Needs must.

Perhaps the interviewer sensed his hesitance.

'Tell me, George. Do you like people?'

'Of course,' said George. 'As long as they're likeable.'

The interviewer laughed at what George presumed was a funny memory that'd just popped into her mind, because he had certainly not made any jokes. She flicked the pen repeatedly against the desk, the way people do when they want to let you know that they're thinking.

'I wouldn't normally do this, given your lack of experience but… your reference was impeccable, and this vacancy really needs filling.'

George wasn't sure what a reference was. Had he given one? He didn't think so. But maybe that was just how things worked in the big city. People were happy to ring up and tell other people you were great. He could see how that would be a pull factor.

'Plus you've got an honest face. That really helps in this gig.'

Nobody had ever said that about George. His mum never was one for compliments. Only instructions. Even her deathbed words sounded like a litany, inconveniently interrupted mid-flow by rigor mortis. Was it a shopping list? Chores to be completed? George wasn't sure. She'd said it all in a tongue from the old country that she'd never bothered to teach him. He probably should've asked. Too late now. Either way, it'd made him feel funny inside, like when you watch a foreign movie without subtitles but can still tell that everyone's sad.

He was glad, though, to hear this about his face because, until he got to know Gloucester better, he imagined he'd be lying to people all the time. Most of them would be holidaymakers so wouldn't have a clue if you were making things up anyway. Nobody fact-checks their holiday.

The interviewer got out of her chair and held out her hand for a shake.

'Get out there, George,' she said. 'Get the street into your feet.'

CELEBRITY PSYCHIC CLAIMS MISSING CAFÉ/ BAKERY OWNER IS DEATH CULT GANG LEADER

Exclusive interview by Gustav Brooks

The unlikely story headlined a fading, crumpled newspaper that declared itself to have been voted South West England's Most Trusted Bi-Monthly Paper (2016 & 2018). There was a part of George – the self-educated, proud, discerning part – that knew that reading this story would be bad for his brain. There was, however, another part of George, a part he shared with every inhabitant of planet Earth, that was just really, really, really compelled by unapologetic trash and it was this part that led him in…

> *With many of us still trying to process the traumatic events of January's biker gang invasion, the truth still feels many pieces away from a full picture. One of those missing pieces is the literally missing figure of Allan 'All-Ears' Hogan. Some of you will remember Allan from his time as publican of the Twisted Yarn, where his penchant for themed events was legendary. Hair Metal Thursdays was a staple at the Enquirer offices!*

The Biker Gang Incident! That part wasn't nonsense; George had definitely heard about it, but it had slipped his mind. It felt like ancient history. After all, that was months ago and news moves so fast these days, even if you're far from where it happens.

When an unspecified personal tragedy led to a new career in artisan baking, we all hoped Allan would quickly find his feet again. So we were crushed to hear that he had gone missing following January's incident, one of many victims of that allegedly Satan-worshipping mob. The remembrance cakes left outside his cafe (most of which looked better than Allan's efforts, it must be said) suggested that we were not the only ones mourning.

Now local celebrity psychic Sally Domino – best known for hosting Britain's Most Haunted Second Homes *– claims that the outpouring of sympathy was misplaced. Allan may have had his ear to the ground, but perhaps it was him we should have been keeping an eye on all along...*

'He was definitely one of them,' claimed Domino during our exclusive phone interview. 'Not just one of them, THE one. The head of the snake.'

What led her to this jaw-dropping conclusion?

'I didn't go looking for it. I never really go asking questions of the dead these days, it's not what you do when you're retired. But there I was hanging upside down, retiling my garage ceiling, when one of the victims came to

me and whispered 'Baker Biker Boss' over and over, and I
knew I had to investigate. After that, it was pretty easy to
put two and two together.'

I asked Ms Domino if Allan not appearing to have ever
owned a motorbike would have limited his participation in
a biker gang. She greets my query with a scoff.

'If anything, that just proves it. The real leaders of
these things don't do any of the driving, do they. Do they?'

The jury, as they say, is out.

George laughed. He didn't intend to. He didn't realise
how much he'd been needing it. He laughed so much that
his chest hurt. Pulled a muscle maybe. Or maybe it was
guilt from laughing when his mum never would again.

George finished his coffee and pushed the paper aside.
He wondered who had left it there. Was it someone still
in this café? Had they laughed too and wanted to share?
Or were they just in a rush?

Life here seemed like that to George. Always a rush.
Like you're chasing someone you don't know. No lives in
the city are new, he decided. You're always just expanding
to fill the cracks someone else left behind. Even your
laughs are second-hand.

Property For Sale: 2-bedroom 4th-floor flat, quayside adjacent in an attractive modern block. Fashionable open-plan layout with exposed brickwork. Presented 'as is' with tasteful contemporary furniture. (Some window restoration work required). Motivated seller. Please contact OLIVER at Big Panda Estate Agents.

Oliver wasn't how George expected him to be. He had been expecting a hustler, that was what estate agents naturally felt like in his mind. And it was possible that the attitude Oliver had on him was part of his own style of hustle, but George reasoned that a hustle should probably make you want to stay. The flat was a bomb site.

'Did something… *happen* here?' asked George, understanding perfectly that the art of playing detective is all in the placement of the dramatic pause.

Oliver shrugged. 'Not as far as I know.'

'I just mean… it's very cheap.'

'You know what?' said Oliver, settling onto the sofa. 'I'd call it a bargain!'

'Suspiciously cheap.'

Judging from Oliver's twitchy response, he had some sort of allergy to the word 'cheap'. To George, this was a good indicator that he should keep using it. 'I'm just learning what I can about this city, but I'm pretty sure this place shouldn't be this cheap.'

A deep sigh from the sofa.

'Look, I don't love it either, mate. I'm on commission, after all. But the seller picked this place up at auction and they're looking to get rid right away. In fact, she told me this morning that it should go to the next person who looked. Lucky you.'

That really *was* lucky.

'If it makes you feel better, you must be paying more than they did.'

It did make him feel better. Somehow, paying much more for property than it used to be worth a mere heartbeat ago felt like communing with an ancient British tradition. He made an offer right away.

George built his routine here over the next few weeks. In the days, he repainted the walls, repaired the window (how *did* a ball smash through all the way up here?) and memorised maps of the city with their corresponding histories. At night, he'd walk the routes he'd studied, layering his learning onto reality. Getting the street into his feet. It was A Lot. If you're really paying attention to detail, you can spend a lifetime studying just one place and you still wouldn't know it all. George had opted to try.

Then there was the stuff in the flat. The former owners had left *so much* behind. Most of it he liked and found to suit him. Even the bum indentation in the sofa seemed to match his own contours very nicely.

But the photos were different. A man. A woman. Smiling. Always smiling! Well… him *trying* to smile and her knowing how to better than anyone George had ever known. It was a smile that let you know everything would be OK and hopefully this couple were, even if the circumstances of George's being there seemed to suggest otherwise. What do you do with abandoned memories? George tossed them. He felt like they were mocking him. 'This is the life you would've had, George,' they seemed to say, 'if you'd moved to the city before you were seventy-nine. What were you hiding from? Look at you now. Old and alone.'

George could do precisely nothing about the first of those things. But he could do something about the second.

WILSON-SOLDADO, Marcia – Three marriages. Two surnames. One heck of a lady. Wednesday nights at Seniors' Hackysack won't be the same without you. Love from all of the girls at Stitchin' Witches to our Martyr of the Cathedral Green.

P.S. We are looking after Mittens best we can. We don't think she realises you're gone yet but might do when the posh food runs out.

It seemed strange to call this place a 'cat home'. No cats would ever find their home here, it was at best a passing residence, a 'cat hotel' or 'cat inn' if you preferred. Sonia, behind the counter, received this rumination from George as if it wasn't the 700th time she'd heard it from a potential adopter; sometimes expressed as a joke, sometimes as a genuine revelation. Today she felt it was the latter. She dutifully nodded at the profundity of the observation and led George along the rows of cages. A small tabby with big ears caught his attention. 'That's Mittens,' said Sonia, unlocking the cage. 'I'll leave you to get acquainted.'

Mittens looked him right in the eyes. *What a delightful, fearless creature!* George thought as the cat scampered towards him and presented her paw. So *very* forward. And yet George couldn't help but take this offer. This was a gesture of love.

Ow.

No. That was a swipe.

Pulling away, George sucked at the blood newly released from the back of his hand when he noticed a woman a few feet away, leaning in to his moment with Mittens. He found himself surprisingly defensive about it. 'Excuse me, ma'am, were you wanting to look at this cat?'

The woman frowned. 'Nah. She's all yours. TARDIS is no place for a kitty. She'd get all over the place. Upside down, more often than not. Imagine the litter tray issues!'

George had never heard of Tardis, but assumed it was a part of Gloucester he'd not gotten to yet. Probably where the 'cool kids' hung out. He filed it in the back of his brain as another place to investigate.

But something was familiar about this woman dressed in blue.

'Have we met before?' he asked. She seemed to take this question very seriously. 'It's perfectly possible,' she said. 'I tend to get about. But I left Gloucester a long time ago. Or not that long ago actually. Depends how you look at it.'

George was not sure how to look at it.

'I just like to check back from time to time, whisper in the right ears, help out some lost souls. Plenty of them about. How about you? Where are you from?'

'Well…' said George. And he realised he had never been asked this question before. How lucky he had been, never having to consider if his appearance matched his location. How wonderful it was to be certain of your belonging. How debilitating, how unsettling it must be to not be able to know, perhaps to never know what the truth of you is.

Although.

Did George know the truth about himself? Come to think of it, he never had asked his mum how they came to be in the middle of nowhere, basically by themselves, for what must have been decades. Centuries? Life just keeps going, even if you're not counting. Was he certain that he was fifty-three years old? Was this face his face? Was that blood from his hand actually green or was it just the lighting in here? Where even *was* the old country? Was he *absolutely sure* that he was human?

George didn't share any of this with the woman, of course. Only one thing needed saying, the answer to the question which felt so obvious when it came. The most certain thing he'd ever felt, maybe the *only* certain thing.

'Me?' He gently lifted Mittens as he spoke, pulling her wary form into a cradle in his chest. A temporary residence, right by his heart, that would one day build itself into a home. 'I'm from around here.'

The woman smiled and, right then, George knew exactly who she was and that everything would be OK.

10

Press Play

by Pete McTighe

The Doctor was feeling lonely. Most of the time, she could suppress those feelings and distract herself by saving a planet, averting a war, or emergency-deep-freezing Krynoid hatchlings. But not today. Today was different.

Today, she sat on the steps of the TARDIS console room, munching her last custard cream, watching the glowing control crystal rise and fall.

Rise and fall.

Rise and fall.

While her space-time machine was in Artron II Recharge Mode, the Doctor couldn't allow anyone else on board, especially humans – the Artron pulses played havoc with their DNA. She guiltily remembered that time with David Bowie, when his left pupil permanently dilated.

The Doctor sighed, savouring her final mouthful of biscuit. Her brain was still working thirteen million to the dozen, in the background, backing up like the biggest and best hard drive in the universe, but it felt dulled and distant. If mardy was an emotion, she was feeling it.

Then the TARDIS beeped. A friendly, quirky little sound she hadn't heard before. It was like it knew what she was thinking (which, of course, it secretly did). Curious, the Doctor scrambled to her feet, and in response a jet of steam hissed out of the console. Projected onto the steam was a line of old Gallifreyan text:

You have one unread message.

'What message?' the Doctor blurted out loud. 'Since when did you start taking messages?'

Since ages ago, the TARDIS replied in a petulant series of hums and whistles.

'Well, aren't you chatty! Where were you last September when I ran out of monologues?'

Just read the message, the TARDIS seemed to say.

The Doctor jabbed a button on the console, then turned as a hologram fizzed into life. She felt a surge of emotion as she stared into the face before her.

The girl was in her mid-teens, with a shock of jet-black hair, a striped top and eyes twinkling with mischief. The sight of her cracked the Doctor's dark mood like an egg.

'Hello, Grandfather,' said the hologram.

The Doctor's voice caught in her throat. 'Hello, Susan,' she finally replied. This was clearly a recording made when her granddaughter was still a teenager. When they were travelling together, so many lifetimes ago.

Susan's image crackled as she continued talking: 'I've built a message bank and retrieval system into the TARDIS data core, for a rainy day. In case you need cheering up. I know what you're like when you get bored, or lonely.'

'What am I like?' snapped the Doctor defensively.

'Grumpy,' Susan replied.

The Doctor clutched her braces and frowned.

'I know nothing lasts forever,' Susan continued, 'and that eventually we'll have to say goodbye. But when that day comes, I want to leave you with some memories of our time together.'

The Doctor's eyes misted over. There was a lump in her throat.

'Not just of me, but of future friends. Future times and places. I've activated the TARDIS record mode, telepathically linked to your data extract. So if you're ever feeling bored, or lonely, or sad, all you have to do is access the databank, and retrieve a favourite memory. It'll keep on recording until you tell it to stop. All your adventures, all your stories won't go to waste. They'll always be here, waiting for you, like an archive. Alive for eternity.'

Stunned, the Doctor watched a stream of text appearing on the screen. Old adventures, logged in a long list that seemingly scrolled forever.

'Some of the early ones might have gaps, sorry about that. You know what the TARDIS is like with integrating new systems.'

The TARDIS grumbled disapprovingly.

'Anyway, I'd better go or I'll be late for school. I hope this message gets to you someday. When you need it most.'

With a final smile, Susan's image flickered, then evaporated. The Doctor stared at the empty space for a very long time. Seconds, at least. Then she snapped into action, scrolling through the endless list of titles, unsure where to begin. 'Crisis on Poosh', 'Genesis of the Daleks', 'Attack of the Postmen', 'The Timelash', '100,000 BC aka An Unearthly Child aka The One in the Stone Age'.

'Intelligent labelling system's a bit random,' thought the Doctor, her finger hovering over the activation button. Finally, she made her selection – and pressed PLAY.

The TARDIS console pinged again. Result! The custard creams had been replenished! The Doctor eagerly plucked one from the dispenser and settled back to watch hazy images form on the screen.

As she chewed, she decided she'd FaceTime Graham, Ryan and Yaz later, but for now she was happily distracted with the gift that Susan had left behind: an endless supply of stories; a comfort blanket of fond memories and old friends.

And a reminder.

That she was never, ever alone.

11

The Shadow Passes

by Paul Cornell

The Doctor had brought them to Calapia for its rural charm, beautiful weather and magnificent ruins. The Calapians, she'd told Yaz, were 'a wonderful bunch, throw a party at the drop of a hat, six heads, lots of hats'. She'd also said they didn't like to talk about the ruins, and a bit later she'd added that she'd never figured out why, two facts which Yaz had placed in the drawer in her head marked, 'Well, I hope that doesn't bite us in the bottom'.

Calapia had turned out to be as advertised: rural; charming; beautiful and magnificent. But the Calapians had been nowhere to be found. As Yaz and her friends had explored the buildings in one of the planet's major cities – buildings which looked like they'd had people in them yesterday, people who'd left and carefully locked their doors behind them – Yaz had thought to herself that that mental drawer of hers got opened a lot. That there wasn't actually a lot left in there, because most of the things that she'd suspected would bite her and her friends in the bottom actually had.

She'd been thinking that when Graham had found the sign. It had said, the letters wobbling a little in the way that indicated the TARDIS was translating for them, 'This way to the shelters'.

'Am I overreacting,' Graham had said, 'or is that just a tiny bit worrying?'

Which was how they'd ended up in a bare room, one hundred feet underground, sitting in a circle, with the names of famous people stuck to their foreheads.

The Calapian who'd opened the door of the shelter when they'd knocked on it had been shocked to find there were still tourists who didn't know about the Death Moon that passed over the planet every 64 years. They had quickly ushered the Doctor and friends inside and had assigned them a room. They'd asked if they had any hats and had seemed pleasantly surprised when they hadn't. Hat storage alone, they'd said, was taking up a whole corridor down here.

'How long's it going to be? I mean, this is a moon, that'll come and go in a night, yeah?' Ryan had asked.

The Calapian had looked awkward on all six of its faces. Then it had told them they would be down here for three of their Earth weeks. There were only minutes before the passage would begin. They had had no hope of getting back to the TARDIS.

'Brilliant,' the Doctor had said, a word which had been completely at odds with the sort of words Yaz had been about to utter. It hadn't matched the looks on the faces of Graham and Ryan either. 'Three weeks of indoor games! Result!'

It had become clear almost immediately that the Doctor, though she liked the idea of indoor games, didn't actually know the rules of many. She'd had in her pocket a chess set, and she could play that, except she insisted on making individual noises for each piece when she moved. She'd also had a travel set of a game she insisted was really called 'Scaribble', despite what it said on the box, because that was how they pronounced it on a planet the name of which she couldn't herself pronounce. They'd tried to play that first, but the Doctor kept putting down letter tiles which formed the names of places and beings she'd known, or just to make a pattern on the board. Then she'd rearrange other people's tiles to suit that pattern and after half a day of that Graham had declared he was going on strike. He went to find the facilities, and came back reporting that, to everyone's relief, things in that department were much like they were at home.

So the Doctor had asked them what they'd like to play. Ryan had played the game with the names stuck on foreheads at parties when he was younger, and if there was one thing the Doctor had in her pockets it was pens, as well as a handy gadget that could manufacture something like paper. 'Except it decays into compost after a day. Or if it doesn't it becomes, you know, highly explosive.'

Which was how they'd come to be all sitting in that circle.

From where she was, Yaz could see that the Doctor had a note reading 'Lewis Capaldi' stuck to her forehead, Graham had 'Mel and Sue' and Ryan had 'Theodoric the Great'. She, of course, had no idea what was stuck to her own forehead. Though whatever it was clearly delighted Ryan and Graham, who'd come up with it between them.

'All right,' said Ryan. 'So, am I… alive?'

The Doctor looked alarmed. 'D'you think you might not be?'

'Is this person alive?' Ryan pointed to his piece of paper.

'Wait, when is this?' said Graham. 'I mean, when is now? 'Cause we'll have to put down a rule to mean—'

'Is this person,' continued Ryan, 'alive in 2020?'

'That's a terrible impersonation,' said the Doctor.

'What?'

'Of him on the piece of paper. You sound nothing like him.'

'Ah,' said Graham, nudging Ryan, 'it's a him.'

Ryan pointed again at the piece of paper and paced his next sentence like there was a social media handclap between every word. 'I don't know who I am.'

'Bit soon for that,' said the Doctor, 'we've only been here one day.'

It ended up being one of the longest party games Yaz had ever taken part in. Or maybe it just felt that way. Following Ryan's painful discovery of the history of the late Roman empire and a bit of confusion about what the word 'goth' meant in that context, Graham's correct guess about how he could be two people at once, and the Doctor's anecdotes about playing the triangle for the 'lovely Scottish lad and his dad', Yaz decided to make a serious attempt to deduce whose name she was wearing. 'Am I a woman?' she said.

'Yes,' said Ryan and Graham quickly and immediately.

Yaz glanced over to see the Doctor open and close her mouth, as if deciding not to say something. Yaz wasn't sure she'd ever seen the Doctor make that decision before.

'OK. Am I famous?'

'Yeah, pretty much,' said Ryan and Graham but, again, the Doctor looked as if she had a problem with that but didn't quite want to voice it.

That, thought Yaz, was unique. Unique was where answers lived. One of her criminology lecturers had said that. Who wasn't the Doctor sure about? To the point where she wasn't even willing to commit to them being a particular gender? Oh. She pointed at the Doctor. 'I'm you,' she said.

Ryan and Graham shouted in defeat, and the Doctor smiled an enormous smile, like sunshine through clouds.

Shortly after, the Doctor fixed all their phones so they could follow stuff from home and added lots of games to them too, though a lot of them didn't make much sense. The prospect of being shut up in here with her slowly changed from, as Ryan had put it in a whisper, 'like being stuck in a lift with a bee' to something a lot more relaxing. Yaz watched, fascinated, as she changed how she acted, almost every hour, just happening to start telling a relaxing, funny story as the night arrived, or turning out her pockets to find miniaturised books. Every now and then she would take herself off for a brisk walk around the room with one or the other of them when they needed to vent or just needed the exercise.

At one point, a small automated device arrived, carrying a basic meal of local fruit and what turned out to be a sort of bread. The Doctor used the sonic screwdriver to confirm they could eat it. Yaz noticed her sizing them all up as they did so, while they talked about what they'd do when they got home, a frown on her face, as if just for a second they'd disappointed her.

A little later that same day, Yaz joined the Doctor on one of her walks. She wanted to share what she'd observed. 'I thought you said you were socially awkward?' she said. ''Cause I'm not seeing that right now.'

The Doctor looked worried. 'I am. Often. Seriously. But this is a task. I'm good at tasks. Thanks for noticing. Don't tell the others. I don't want them to start seeing me doing it. Or they'll get tired too.'

'You made yourself annoying so we'd feel relieved when you stopped.'

'Oh. Yeah. Did that without thinking about it. Relief that summat's better than you thought it would be will get you through a day or so of awfulness. I learned that at Woodstock.'

'Do you do that a lot?'

'What, go to 1960s hippy rock festivals? No. Never again. The mud. The poetry. The nudity. Or was that the Somme?'

'I mean make yourself look smaller than you are.'

The Doctor's face gurned as it only did when her brain was wrestling with something she didn't particularly enjoy considering. 'S'pose. I used to like it when people underestimated me, but in this body it's a bit rubbish, because when I go "Aha!" and I want people to stop underestimating me, they just keep right on underestimating me.'

Yaz felt that. 'We don't do that, though. None of us. I sometimes think if we could see all you were, at once, it'd be too much. We couldn't deal.'

The Doctor looked bashful and pleased all at the same time, which was another of Yaz's favourite looks of hers. 'Well, I certainly can't. I'm a bit too much for me. I'm more than I knew about. Still processing all that. I sometimes think that's why I change personality instead of just making my body younger. I need to switch myself off and on again so I can handle all the memories, so a lot of it feels like it happened to someone else. I get a different perspective on what I've done. I've been thinking a lot about that lately. There's this girl in a mirror. Where I put her. That doesn't suit who I am now. When we get out of here… Oh, this is getting deep and meaningful, isn't it?' Yaz was about to say that was fine, but the Doctor swung to include the others, suddenly pulling another surprise from her pockets. 'Balloon animals!'

Graham raised his hand, which was half a request and half an order for the Doctor to halt. 'I've been thinking,' he said, 'about where that meal came from. I think we should go find some Calapians and say thanks.'

'Yeah,' said Ryan, 'see if we can help out.'

And there on the Doctor's face, Yaz saw that enormous smile again.

And so the days passed in balloon animals and yoga and karaoke and also in learning all sorts of things about what Calapians liked to do, as the Doctor and her friends cooked and distributed alongside them.

On the last night of the passing of the Death Moon, everyone in the shelter came together and ate and was quiet, and all those heads lowered in remembrance of what had gone and those who'd been lost. The heads of the Doctor and her friends were lowered with them.

Yaz felt, by the end of it, that she'd had a rest, honestly, physically and spiritually. Something had been proven to her in isolation. The Doctor saw that look on her face as they waited for the big doors to open. 'In the midst of death,' she said, so gently that only Yaz could hear it, 'we are in life. Together.'

The doors opened and they stepped out into the daylight. Graham and Ryan grabbed each other and laughed.

Yaz took a deep breath. And the air was good.

12

Shadow of a Doubt

by Paul Cornell

In the ruins of Andromeda, I found a mirror from old Earth. It had survived far longer than a mirror should. It was made of interesting and suspicious materials. I kept it in my tent. One night, in the mirror appeared a little girl with a balloon. I had good reason to be afraid. I'd known a girl like that. I'd been hunted by a girl like that. But this wasn't quite her. And she didn't seem frightening. There was something broken about her. She asked me if I was him. I'd have replied with something cutting, but she looked so sad in that moment. She told me that he, or often she, had kept visiting her, once a year, forever. There had been the old one with all the hair. He had been the worst. There had been the one I travelled with. He had been the worst too. There had been the thin white aristocrat and the one who couldn't walk and the one

143

with the red hair who thought he was the last. But they'd kept coming. They always asked the same question. They asked her if she was sorry. She'd tried so many different things. She'd asked them how she could be sorry for a story that had happened many times in many ways. She hadn't even been present for all of them. She could see that from inside the mirror. They'd told her *they* were a story that had happened many times in many ways and they would not excuse her. All she had to do was say sorry. But she could not bring herself to. She told me she was incapable of it. But the look in her eye when she said it made me not believe it. She asked me to let her out, then. She asked me to do what he would not. As I often have. I asked her if she was sorry for what she did to me. She tried to tell me that was a different her. I said that was a story I'd heard before. I said she'd lived far longer than she should have and had learned nothing. I returned the mirror to the ruins where he would find it. I came back that way a few years later and it had gone. I don't know if she ever got out. Perhaps he returned her, in the end, to where he found her. To all the places he'd found her. Long ago, in an English spring.

13

Shadow in the Mirror

by Paul Cornell

I don't know how long I was in the mirror for. Centuries, at least. I saw the Doctors on a regular basis. They found me no matter what mirror I was exploring that day. Some of them didn't even seem to remember much about me. But they had always demanded I say sorry. They said they'd release me if I did. I always refused. Because I wasn't sorry. Then they went away.

Until one day a new Doctor found me. She hadn't visited me before. She had a swoop of blonde hair and a great seriousness about her, despite the fact that she wore a costume with a rainbow across her chest that said she liked to entertain children. On her lapel she wore a badge of a white poppy. 'So the red-headed Doctor was wrong,' I said. 'He wasn't the last.'

She told me she didn't know about that. But that one rule, perhaps the only solid rule, of being the Doctor was that Doctors didn't know much about themselves. She said she had come here to break another rule, a rule about crossing her own future, about changing decisions her other selves had made and were going to make. Because she thought it was a rule that should be broken. She'd been locked in with some friends somewhere. She'd considered her sins. She'd decided there were several sicknesses in her that needed curing. She asked me if I still wanted to get out.

'Of course,' I said. 'But if you've come to gloat, you should know I haven't suffered. I've been to every mirror in the universe and I've frightened many children. I will not bow to you. I will not say sorry. Ever.'

She said she understood that. That in many ways it was her own fault that myself and my family had killed so many people.

That made me scream at her. 'What I did wasn't up to you!'

She told me what I already knew, that if she released me from the mirror I'd have a life of days or weeks, my normal lifetime, starting again from the point where it had been suspended.

'I still want to get out,' I said. 'But I will not say sorry. My family did what they needed to do. What they were born to do. If you let me out I'll keep on killing lesser beings and then you'll have that on your conscience too.'

She asked me if I knew what mercy was. I wouldn't reply. She said then that mercy had nothing to do with fairness. That mercy set fairness aside and said there was no getting even, no balancing the scales. There was only deciding against pain. There was only being kind to yourself by being kind to others. She said she didn't need me to be sorry.

And she took a big hammer from her pocket.

I jumped back from the mirror as she smashed it. She smashed it time after time, smashed it into a million pieces. Then she held out her hand to me. The expression on her face was stern, not welcoming. She said something about this being an end to bad luck.

I didn't take her hand. But I did step out of the mirror.

She said there was nothing on this world. That was why she'd come to free me here. She took me to her TARDIS. She stayed looking determined as she operated the controls. She watched me in case I touched anything. I was shaking inside, trying to deal with my freedom, hoping against hope this wasn't some further twist on her revenge.

When the doors opened, there was my home. There were the spires and the great spiral troughs. There were my people, linking in the great chains, sunning themselves on the rocks in their natural form.

She told me to get out. She told me that I wouldn't have time to leave this place before the end of my natural life. That I would be free to live and die as I should have in the first place. That she had made this decision for me and for herself and for all her other selves.

I stepped out of the doors. I was really there. Really home. I didn't understand why she'd done that. I still don't. I was furious at her for having this power over me. As my people are always angry because of the historical injustices perpetrated against us. I was about to turn and release my balloon to eat her face.

But by the time I did so, her TARDIS had already faded away.

I could only turn back to look at my world. I couldn't help but feel something relax inside me at being back in the embrace of my people. They were already coming towards me, calling out, curious, welcoming.

I took a deep breath. And the air was good.

14

Fellow Traveller

by Mark Gatiss

It was probably a Tuesday. That's what I thought as I made my way up the old road. *Road* was pushing it, to be honest; it was little more than a dirty track with the hedgerows crowding in from the sides so that they formed a sort of dark green tunnel. No vehicles had been along that road for a long time, you see. And probably very few people.

But I shrugged the little rucksack further up my back and trudged on, my new boots squelching through liquid brown mud. I'd liberated the boots from a shattered shop window display in a building still scorched from long-gone gunfire: mannequins stood limbless and broken, and a wren had made a rough nest in the corner. I spent a happy afternoon there trying on dresses just for the hell of it. I couldn't remember the last time I'd worn one.

Maybe that evening we'd pretended like none of it had happened. Imagined what it might have been like if we'd met under normal circumstances… But the boots – the boots were sturdy and still sound so I took them. No one would mind.

It was quite easy making my way across country. The weather was pretty good and there were plenty of dry, warm barns and outhouses still standing. Occasionally, I even found whole farms intact. As I headed north, I lost track of the days. But I thought it was a Tuesday.

Come to think of it, it was probably a Tuesday when *they* came.

I was avoiding the big towns, of course. There'd been some effort to get them up and running again, but the rats were everywhere, growing in size and confidence, and most people were happier out in the countryside, making a go of the new settlements which were more like medieval villages. Simple, functional and, on the whole, working.

I was somewhere on the outskirts of what was left of Luton when I saw her.

It had started to rain, that sort of fine, cold, annoying rain that doesn't seem like much but ends up leaving you drenched. The sky above the looming hillside was a sort of brilliant, electric grey, as though a storm were coming. And suddenly there was a figure there, silhouetted like a

scarecrow. A long grey coat with the hood up and stout boots like mine. As I trudged closer, the figure produced, as if from nowhere, a battered umbrella and put it up.

'Going my way?' she said, letting the umbrella cover me.

'Thanks.'

She craned her neck to peer towards the hill. 'There's a farmhouse close by, I think. Abandoned. We could stop there for a bit, if you like. Get out of the rain.' I couldn't see much of her face because of the hood but a big grin split her rain-dimpled face. 'And – I've got sandwiches!' she enthused. 'Cheese and pickle. *Branston*, obvs. It's not much but you're welcome to share. Come on.'

She thrust the umbrella into my hand and clomped on, the mud adding inches to the soles of her boots.

'There now,' the stranger said. 'That's better. Isn't that better?'

Somehow she'd got a fire going and the tiny old front room of the farmhouse, its flock wallpaper peeling, its furniture bursting and damp, felt almost cosy. Through the grimy windows, I could see that night was coming on and I was grateful to be inside with a friend.

Friend? I knew nothing about her. She knelt down by the fire, rubbed her hands together cheerfully and finally pulled back the hood of her coat. Her blonde hair was damp and stuck to her forehead and her eyes were bright in the firelight. When she talked, which was often, her nose crinkled up in a sort of sulky frown before the big, sloppy grin reasserted itself.

'This is very kind of you,' I said at last. 'Taking pity on an old woman.'

'Old? You? You're not old! I was just thinking how good you looked. Can't have been easy. All these years. How long has it been… actually?' The nose crinkled up again.

'Since what?'

'Since the defeat. Since you all sent them packing.'

I shrugged. 'Must be… fifty years. More. It's easy to lose track and since…' I felt myself go all hot and my chest tighten. 'Since… well, lately I've become a bit of a hermit.'

The woman was sitting with her legs crossed now, like a cobbler in a fairy tale. She had on a T-shirt, damp with rain like everything else, with a faded rainbow on it. That made me smile. 'But you're not being a hermit now, are you?' she said. 'You're out and about!'

'Yes.'

'Heading… where?'

'North,' I said quietly. 'Unfinished business. Did you say something about sandwiches? I'm starving.'

She held up a hand, like a magician about to perform a particularly brilliant trick, and produced a parcel of sandwiches (wrapped in grease-proof paper in the old fashioned way) from her capacious pockets. The bread was fresh and delicious. And there was tea! Tea in a flask.

'You know,' I said at last, after eating my fill. 'We haven't even introduced ourselves—'

'This unfinished business of yours,' said the stranger, cutting across me. 'Can I help out at all?'

I smiled, shook my head. 'I don't think so. It's just something I… I have to do.'

'Where?'

'Bedford.'

'Bedford! What a coincidence! I'm heading that way. Bedford's great! Haven't been to Bedford in yonks. Why Bedford?'

I looked into the fire and watched the damp sticks pop and spark. 'I heard there were still some of… them left there. If you look hard enough. There was a great purge, you see. After it was all over. People just wanted to forget. So all the remains were collected together. Thousands and thousands of them. Put into a great heap and burned in Trafalgar Square. Victory Day.' I shrugged. 'Cathartic, I suppose. People needed that. Needed to feel we'd properly won.'

'So… why…?'

'I'm a widow now. And there are things… feelings that I need to let out. Let go of. My husband was a good man. We worked well together.' I smiled a small smile. '*Most* of the time. But it was hard. So very hard. And it was because of *them* that his life was shorter than it should have been. The strain eventually… wore him out. I just… need to see one again.'

She bowed her head. The reflected flames danced in her dark eyes. 'I'm very sorry for your loss.'

I passed a hand over my eyes. I suddenly felt very tired and very old. 'Do you know,' I said, 'I think I'll get my head down. We've a long walk in the morning.'

The stranger nodded vigorously. 'Right. Yes. Absolutely. There's probably a nice warm bed made up for you upstairs. Probably.'

And you know what? There was.

I don't know if it was because the rain had cleared, whether it was just the freshness of a new day (Wednesday, we must suppose) or the incredible smell of kippers (*kippers!*) coming from downstairs, but I woke up feeling cheerful. Properly cheerful in a way I hadn't felt for a very long time.

I struggled back into my clothes (which seemed to have been warmed and aired) and went quietly down the winding staircase of the farmhouse.

My new friend was bent over the cooker, a pan of kippers in one hand, pouring out tea from an old brown pot with the other. She beamed when I appeared.

'Hiya! Hope this OK. It's amazing what you can find when you have a root about. Whoever used to live here knew how to live.'

I found this very doubtful. Kippers didn't tend to survive global emergencies. But maybe I'd already guessed by then that my new friend was something unusual.

'You're full of surprises,' was all I said.

'Aren't I just?'

'I can't let you do all this. Wait on me hand and foot. Please, let me—'

'Don't even think about it.' She propelled me to the battered old kitchen table. 'My treat. You've been through the mill. You deserve a bit of TLC.'

And she touched my head tenderly.

Then she served up the kippers and the tea and a great big pile of fresh bread and butter. Knife and fork in hand, she sat down at the head of the table. 'I've got another surprise for you too. It's in the barn.'

'What is?'

She pushed a stray strand of blonde hair from her face. 'I'll show you after breakfast. Come on. Tuck in.'

The barn was very old. A high, beamed ceiling. Crumbling farm tools rusted against the walls and there were still scraps of slimy straw in the corners. As my friend heaved open the door, they lifted into the air in little whirls of dust.

In the middle of the barn was a shape, covered in a battered green tarpaulin. I shuddered. Even after all these years, it was all too familiar. 'You're not trying to tell me,' I said incredulously, 'that you just… found one lying about?'

'Yeah!' she cried brightly. 'Well… no. No, not exactly. I had to, you know, root about for it a bit. Like the kippers.'

'Some kipper.' I gazed very levelly at her. 'Tell me the truth. Where *did* you find it?'

'I told you!'

'The *truth.*'

She looked away, shrugged, plunged her hands into the pockets of her long coat. Her nose screwed up again. 'Bedford.'

'*Bedford?*'

'Yeah. What you heard was right. There are still a few lying about. Bits and bobs. Blown-up ones full of rain water. A couple smashed in half right next to the old mine where…'

She stopped. Looked right at me with dark brown eyes which once were blue. And I shivered.

Then I pulled back the tarpaulin.

It was smaller than I remembered. Long dead. Disfigured. The domed head had been almost entirely crushed in, the arm and the gun were missing, and the bulky lower half blossomed with rust and mould.

I felt something being placed into my hand. It was a big length of steel broken off from a girder. The stranger was holding something similar.

She smiled. 'You know, it's important to have a good cry. Let things out. Stamp your feet and shout your head off. Especially when you've lost someone. But sometimes… *sometimes* you just really need to bash a Dalek with a big stick.' She gestured to me. 'After you.'

I took a deep breath. Lifted the steel bar high over my head. And then it all came pouring out. All the years of struggle. Hardship. Homesickness. Abandonment. And the grief. Oh God, the stabbing, vicious, crushing grief.

I brought down the bar and it connected with the Dalek's head with the most satisfying of crunches. 'This…' I gasped. '*This* is for David.'

I didn't make much of an impression on it, of course. Their armour was pretty invincible, except, perhaps, to the ravages of time. And I'm a geriatric with little fighting energy left in her. At least in this incarnation. I suppose this old body of mine *is* wearing a bit thin. And now, with David gone, perhaps it's time for new horizons. New adventures.

Afterwards, the stranger and I sat by a stream and listened to its musical tinkle and splash. A beautiful sound. The sun was high in a bright sky as blue as a cornflower.

'I thought I'd made a new friend,' I said. 'But it turns out you're an old one. My oldest. More than that. *Family*.'

'When did you know?' she asked.

'Probably… probably the kippers.'

The stranger laughed. 'You always liked them, didn't you? Used to make me pop out for them. When we were in the junkyard.'

'Well, the food machine could never quite get the flavour right. Tasted all chocolatey.'

She looked me up and down. 'You haven't changed a bit.'

'*You* have!'

'Yeah, well, you know. It's a lottery. But it was about time.'

I sighed. 'Everything is.'

'We have a lot to catch up on, don't we?'

'That we do.'

She stood up, and I let her put her arm around me. It was so familiar that my eyes pricked with tears.

'You see, my dear,' she said, 'I always told you I'd come back.'

15

Listen

by Steven Moffat

What's that in the mirror?
And the corner of my eye?
What's that footstep following?
And never passing by?

At night I hear such breathing
The dark is never still
The shadows all are seething
The air is damp and chill

Even as I write this
The shadows all have moved
How do I learn to fight this?
This enemy unproved

And now a voice is muttering
A voice that's not my own
The candle now is guttering
The wind is now a moan

And wait, the door is knocking
And no, this can't be right
The door I'm always locking
Is opening tonight

And standing there with blazing eyes
A man I'd never seen
His face was pale and strange and wise
And lined and very lean

'This poem that you're writing
You now must throw away.
The shadows that you're fighting
I fight them every day.'

One night I'll have to read it
And fear will grip my soul.
This fear I do not need it
This fear will take a toll.'

I listened as he ranted
And then I told him no
For words, like seeds, once planted
Towards the light must grow

He stood there now in silence
He did not turn to go
His eyes were full of violence
But his voice was soft and low

'These seeds you must not sow them.
Please cast them on the rocks.
I'm the reader of this poem
I'm a madman with a box.'

16

The Secret of Novice Hame

by Russell T Davies

This is the last day of my life.

They have built a bower for me, here on the clifftops, overlooking the New Atlantic. I'm lying in a cradle of wood and silk. Huge pavilions of white cotton have been raised up, so that people might come and pay their last respects.

The canvas billows in the breeze from the sea; it reminds me of the refugee camps where I was born.

My parents were made homeless when the Mechanical War swept across the Western Arm of the Spiral Conflagration. I was born in the middle of battle, beneath a sky on fire, the last of a litter of 16. My mother and father sold me. Their kittens were starving, so they gave me to the Sisters of Plenitude for ten shillings, enough to buy the rest of my family a berth on the last shuttle out of Restitution. They fled, into the stars. Leaving me behind. And then the Sisters wrapped me in swaddling clothes and took me to New Earth.

I was called Hame, after the Cat God of Harvest. At 13, I was inducted as Novice Hame. And then… Oh, it's such a long story and my time is running short. Though there are recordings, I think, and holograms of my adventures. Such mad days! It's impossible to think, but once, I was such a wildcat, shouldering guns and fighting foes and running alongside a Lord of Time!

But time passed. And responsibilities grew. I sought to atone for the sins of the Sisterhood, becoming Senator Hame. Then Vice President Hame. Then Feline Imperator of the New Earth Order.

Today, I am called Novice Hame once more. Because at my age, every day is new. With so much still to learn.

And I am waiting. At the end of my life, I am still waiting.

For him.

Because I have one, last secret to be told.

Once, it was said of the Face of Boe that, on the day of his death, he would impart a vital secret to a lonely traveller. I think to myself, how strange, and how right, that history should repeat.

But don't think the pavilions are a place of sadness! My life has been one of joy, and luck, and love, I want to be celebrated here! I want children to remember the day they laughed with the funny old cat. So the crowds come, and bask in the bright sunlight, on the sloping hills of apple-grass. There's no need for the Hippopotamus Guard, though they stand on duty nevertheless, spears at the ready. All around them, Dog-kind and Sparrow-forms dart and bark. Swans and Flamingos feed the visitors, carrying platters laden with curds and whey and roasted corn. And as evening sets, the Dolphin Children dance in the firelight.

As the days pass, they approach me, one by one. The Lion-kind bow. The Heron-folk sing songs of the old days. And the little Mice-kind, dressed in tunics of gold and purple, nibble at my paws then run away, still scared of their old enemy, the cat, after five billion years. But the last surviving Owl-woman stands before me and merely blinks. With such wisdom. As though she knows.

I think the owl and the pussycat have always known.

There are traditions to be upheld. In my paw, I clasp two gold coins. They will be taken, by my final visitor, and placed upon my eyes, to pay for my journey into the Great Cat Kingdom beyond. So I wait. For that final visitor's approach.

And now, tonight, the clifftops are asleep. The fires flicker into ash. The crescent moon shines off the water, with the lights of New New York glittering on the horizon. The Hippopotamus Guard stand on duty, but sleeping, held upright by their uniforms of bronze and rope. The encampments of every kind of animal stir and mutter, but drift into dreams. The air is still, as though paused.

I wait.

And then, out of the silence and the darkness…

He comes.

He says, 'Hello.'

He hasn't changed at all. I've heard so many stories about him, over the years: his hundreds of faces and forms; the men and women and animals who have taken that name. And yet, the one who comes to me is so familiar. This one is mine.

I say, 'Doctor.'

And that funny, skinny man sits beside me. My old friend.

He looks around, at the moonlit pavilions stretching away into the distance. 'Well, this is a bit of a fuss, isn't it? What's wrong? Is someone ill?'

And we both laugh.

'Where are you now?' I ask him. 'Where in your life?'

'Oh. I'm on something of a final journey myself. Got a little bit poisoned. Like you do. And everything's about to change, so… I'm just saying goodbye.' He smiles. A vast sadness in his eyes.

My secret must be told. But before that, I have happier things to say. 'A wonderful thing happened, Doctor. My mother and father. They found me. They were so old, but so kind, and they came to New Earth, looking for forgiveness, I said there's nothing to forgive, and we hugged, and…'

I realise he's nodding. Rather too politely. And then I realise it all.

'You found them. You sent them to me.'

He says, 'I might have given them a little nudge.'

I thank him. And hold his hand. The two gold coins in my paw become his.

I ask him, 'Was he right? The Face of Boe? He said, when last we met, he said, you are not alone. Was that true?'

'Oh yes!' said the Doctor, with a grin. 'And that was just the start! Blimey, I've had some times since I last saw you. The things that happened! Where do I begin?'

He draws close, and tells me tales of men and monsters, of scarecrows and statues, of distant drums and ancient floods. He spins yarns and legends all through the night, until I see the first streaks of dawn at the horizon.

But this new day is not for me. I thank the Doctor for his stories, for helping my final hours to pass.

He says, 'If I've done anything good with my life, maybe it's that. The stories I leave behind.' Then he asks me, quietly, 'And what does your religion say, Novice Hame? What happens next? Where does your story go?'

I say, 'The Great Cat Kingdom.'

He says, 'D'you believe it exists?'

I tell him, 'I wonder. That's all I can do. I wonder.'

And then I grip his hand, tight. Because the moment has come. And the secret must be told.

'Did you never think, Doctor? How strange it is, that New Earth exists? By what coincidence, it has exactly the same diameter and air and orbit as the original Earth? Because it drew us here, across the stars, every man and woman and cat and dog and bird and beast and spider-kind. The planet called us home. And we thought it a blessing. But as the years passed, I began to think: what if this happened by design? And that thought led to another. What if this world is not a home? What if it's a trap? A long, slow, careful trap of infinite complexity. So I began to investigate. I looked beneath the surface of this world, and do you know what I found, Doctor? Do you know what I discovered?'

The Doctor says, 'I think she's gone.'

He is placing two gold coins upon my eyes.

I say, 'Doctor? Can you hear me?'

But he's looking up and beyond me, to my attendant, who steps out of the shadows. I hear them, as though from far away. My attendant asks if I had any last words.

'I wonder,' says the Doctor. 'That's what she said. Good for her. It's a fine way to live and a fine way to die, always wondering, right to the end.'

And this is my final realisation. That the secret will have to wait. For other times, other cats, other Doctors.

Because these things are drifting away from me now. All these lords and creatures and apple-grass seem so delicate, and so precious, and so faint. They fall away, these earthly concerns, all that weight and doubt and sensation, falling, and lifting, and dispersing on the breeze.

Dawn floods the world with orange and yellow and white, and I'm a thought now, I'm a whisper, I'm an instinct. I'm hope.

Ending. Or beginning. I don't know.

I rise towards the sky, and I wonder.

I wonder.

Illustrations by